MW01242872

Author Cynthia Amis Dickerson

Cover Photo by Mrs. Diann Kelly of Memphis, Tennessee

MOMMA'S Journey to Hell and Back!

Copyright © 2016 by Cynthia Amis Dickerson

1st Edition

Cover by: Mrs. Diann Kelly of Memphis, Tennessee

ISBN: 978098898872-9

Book Website
www.Cynthiadickerson.com

Printed in U.S.A

Dedications

I WOULD LIKE TO THANK MY ALMIGHTY GOD FOR SELECTING ME TO CARRY THE BANNER OF BREAST CANCER AND TRAVEL THAT JOURNEY AND COME OUT ON THE OTHER SIDE HEALED, BLESSED AND STRONGER. I DEDICATE THIS BOOK TO SURVIVORS AND THE COURAGEOUS ONES WHO LOST THE BATTLE BUT NEVER LOST THEIR FAITH.

To Arlena Dean,
The greatest reviewer of books
and the fastest avid reader
I know. You are such a
wonderful giving person god
to call you friend.
Love ya!
Cynthia Amos Jackson
5/23/16

Momma's Journey to Hell and Back

When I walked down the aisle of the church that Sunday morning, I stripped off most of my good clothes, shoes, and a fancy new wig that exposed my neatly braided up hair style. The pipe I had for years, I just dropped it in the lap of a stunned perfect stranger. I had to have gotten hold to some awful bad dope, or I was losing my freaking mind. I disgraced myself, losing what little dignity I had left when I told all my business in front of a church full of hypocrites, and those do-gooders turned their noses up as I passed, prancing up to the altar. To make matters worse, I called my ig'nant self a crack-head hoe. Wow, I know I have been on drugs a long time but damn, I was on the floor weeping. After ten minutes of crying like a fool, I said to myself, "What the hell am I doing? I am not ready for this. I need to get my stupid self up off this floor. I don't know where I'm goin' but I know I need to get ta steppin' outta here."

What happened next is something I didn't expect; I should have kept my dumb ass in the church. I had just stolen some things from the store near the church. I would not have gotten caught if I hadn't run up in the church. I didn't have church on my mind. I saw Louvious, my son's name, on the sign announcing he was preaching, so something told me to go up in the place and see what was going on. Like magic, I was down the aisle, grabbing my new wig and tossing it in the air and then ripping off my clothes, strolling and stripping up in the sanctuary. I guess I shoulda stayed a little longer 'cause the po-po was searching for me. When I ran out in the street, a blue squad car almost hit me, and before I could look up and take a breath, I was tossed in the back seat of the car. Bad Ass, the neighborhood police officer, cuffed me in a matter of seconds. He didn't read me no rights or ask me no questions. He knew me from other encounters with the law so when the call came in and he saw me running, he arrested me no questions asked.

I was so stunned by being apprehended so fast that I just had nothing to say. I turned and looked over my shoulder out the backseat window and I could see Louvious running out of the side door of the church with his black robe flapping in the wind, wiping that sweat-soaked, once-was-pure, white handkerchief across his big, stupid, cornerstone forehead. He looked so funny looking up and down the street. I laughed so hard;

I guessed he thought God took Momma right on up to heaven. What a screwball! I laughed my head off, ha ha ha ha ha ha ha ha!!!!!!!!!!!!

Chapter One

I am Louvenia Johnson. My life for as long as I can remember has been hard. I had to grow up living with pain and unspoken secrets I could not share and didn't share. Trusting and talking to family folk and even my sister Mabel was not an option. I had to keep things to myself. If you can't trust your own so-called loved ones, who in the hell can you trust? You sho' can't trust those fake ass, Sunday-in-church-all-day-long, so called damn church people. Why does anger and rage flare up inside me so quickly? How did I get to this point in my life? Rage is my friend; most of the time I enjoy cussing out people. When they say something stupid, I just can't let it go. I must speak my mind and if they don't like it, I bust them upside the head without any warning. I really love when they fall to the ground; my feet itch to kick 'em. Ooooh! I really enjoy watching them hold their hands to their head and face. The hollering is what makes me smile, and trembling bodies bring me joy.

Well, I remember being in a small narrow cramped room, over my head, are different objects of various sizes touching my head. When I am crouched down, I am on my knees, playing with long plastic objects that have strings and tiny straps attached to them. The floor and the sides of the room are made of wood and it has a funny musty smell. The odor has a scent like you would whiff in the middle of an open woodsy field with just a hint of peppermint. I play for hours in my favorite little hiding place. I hear a heavy voice; it is my grandfather, and he has two different fragrances, one from his mouth and another from his lower overall pants. He turns the knob, shrinks himself and kneels down moving inside stumbling, almost falling as he moves toward me making a swishing sound with his finger next to his thumb touching his gigantic big, wet, juicy-looking thick lips.

He treats me different when he comes in my hiding space. His touch feels strange when we are in my room. I don't like him when he invades my space; he should not be here. His huge hard scratchy hands are all over my body. He makes sounds I don't understand and his dark eyes are closed. I am confused and I don't understand why he comes to my special place and after the sounds and the new awful smell, he tells me, "This is our secret and if you ever tell anyone I will whup you until red blood is torn from your soft, tender skin."

6

I am taken to the police station, stripped, mug shot taken and fingerprinted. I am questioned. It is a different day and a different offence. Well, well I see some familiar faces as I am walked back to the cell by an ugly bucktooth, granny female guard. I walk in the cell and immediately know that trying to claim a cot near the front is going to be drama. I don't feel like it, so I go straight for one of the back cots. Tall mama, with jacked up red hair, skinny legs, freckled face, two teeth missing, shouts, "That's my bed, Ms. Big Butt." I look at her and move to the next cot. An old woman looking to be about 70 but mo' like 30 slurs out, "That's my cot, Big Butt Cow."

Now, I'm trying not to cause no mo' ruckus, but my eyes start to strain and my breathing slows down and my hands start to tighten. I move to the third cot and a few things are on it; a book, shoes and a jacket, I snatch the blanket and throw all that shit on the floor. The third lady looks up at me in this smelly cell, shouting in a Jamaican voice, "Mane, why you throwing my stuff on the freaking floor? What, you high or crazy? Whatsoever you are, sis, you need to pick up my thangs and place 'em on my bed, fool." She is pointing with her finger, and standing too close to me with spit popping on my neck. Now this cow, as one of them called me, has disrespected me three whole times. I can't back down now, even if I wanted to; this is ass-whupping time.

I get ready to punch the hell out of all these females, and the elderly guard limps to the door of the cell, and says, "Hold up in here; the Psych Doc wants to interview you. Please stop acting crazy in here. Go show the doctor how crazy your ass really is. Please step to the door." I look around and before I could tell them this is not the end of this, they say together, "It's not over. We got you when you bring your big booty back." Tall Mama moves close to me and says, "Believe that, hoe."

When I get older I understand what is happening and I do not go and play or enter that dark creepy closet. I stay away from my grandpa, especially when I am in a room alone with him. The women in the family protect me when grandpa calls for me to come sit on his lap. I slowly shake my head, refusing to move close to him. The women in the family protect me from his smothering embrace. My aunts, older cousins,

7

grandmother and my sister Mabel always usher me from his hugs; they all have the same terrified look I have on my face.

How can a Baptist preacher that all the church people love, have a dark side? Why is he allowed to operate in God's house and everyone knows his desires and sinful life and the so-called saints are silent? What does the Bible say about a corrupt preacher, and the sheep that turn a blind eye? My grandmother always seems to get mad at me when she sees me near her husband. Her gospel songs stop and she glares at me with those fiery, burnt brown eyes staring harshly. I don't get it; these are the times when Granny will say, "Sit your fast little black ass down." Man, I don't get it! What have I done?

I am in the ninth grade at Hillside Junior High. I have sexual urges, rage and desires coexisting, in my head and I don't seem to have control. One minute, I have anger exploding like a volcano, and the next minute I have yearnings that seem to stimulate my impulsive sexual pleasures. I have no control; it is like these two emotions have complete domination over my life. What kind of human cannot restrain or regulate the way they think and feel? How can I not have self-control over my pitiful life?

Within the dark musty gray cement walls in the basement of the school is the place I go to be with a different male, old or young, every Monday, Tuesday, Wednesday, Thursday, Friday, five days a week. I can't help myself and anger escalates after every episode. Knocking over garbage cans, running water in the sink to flood the restroom and cussing anyone in my path is how the rage manifests. What can I do to calm my life after the yearnings have been satisfied and the meanness has surfaced? "I need to get high, get drunk, I need numbness." How can I ever feel at peace and have no urges? I want to go to sleep; I am too jittery; my hands are shaking uncontrollably; feet and legs will not stop moving.

"Ahhhhh, help, help," I scream so loudly. I fall to the cold, grimy floor, weeping, holding my head, snot running from my nose, dripping sticky stuff down my face. My head begins to pound and throb like a heart beating. Just then I hear hundreds of keys clanking and a slow dragging sound. The janitor, Mister Nosey Thompson is coming down the steps. I know it is him because the dragging sound is Nosey's bad leg that, according to him, was injured in Nam.

But everyone knows that his old lady stabbed him in the leg at the juke joint when he was messing with one of her friends. Mr. Nosey Thompson, shouts out, "Girl, get yo' fast tail upstairs and go to class. You are always down here messing around with some boy. Are you some kind of basement freak? You are always down here messing around like you some kind of mole. I know you, with your crazy self, flooded the restroom and knocked over the garbage cans." He points and says, "Take your funky, screwing-every-boy, no reading, lunatic hot butt, away from down here." I look at him and feel so wounded; I can't cuss his old ass out. I can't say a word. I walk slowly up the stairs with a tear stained face. I keep walking up the stairs until I walk straight out of the school through the front door undetected.

I am not sure how I feel. The janitor, who is dumb as nails, just gave me some true checks about myself. He said, "Take your funky, screwing-every-boy, no reading, lunatic hot butt, away from down here." I can't get mad because the fool spoke the truth about me. A boy does not have to say, "You are my girlfriend," "I love or I like you," he just touches the front of the lower part of his pants and the panties are coming off. I gotta do better; it's time to make a change. I got a plan; I will go back to school. As I turn, I see out of the corner of my eye Mr. Fine Fireman and he's looking my way. I will do better next week. OOOH WEEEE!

I see this brown, long, slender morsel of sweet honey looking good in that starched blue uniform, with creases in the pants that would make any crooked line straight. Leon is an older man. I try to cool my hot self off. He walks toward me smiling; my mind says go back to school, but something else says, "Girl, go get you some of that!" He comes over saying, "Baby sister, why are you not in class?" I blurt out before I can think, "I gotta have you." He said, with a frown on his face, "Jailbait, get your hot behind back in that school." I say to him, "Don't you want to roll around with me?" He said with a concerned look on his face. "Why don't you value yourself?" "Man, don't be asking me no questions. What you 'pose to be, a teacher? You just a lousy, thank-you-somebody fireman."
"I value myself and respect myself, so I can't see why you lower yourself by offering your body, like it's God's gift to anybody and everybody. You must first respect yourself."

"Stop, I don't need no preaching from the likes of you. Get outta my face, wannabe somebody daddy, I mean granddaddy. I don't wanna hear nothing else you got ta say. Goodbye and good riddance!"

Leon looks at me, shaking his head and hollers out as I switch off, telling me to have a nice day. I feel like punching him in the face and cussing him out, but I change my mind because sooner or later he will want some of this! I feel a little ashamed when Leon asked, "Why don't you value yourself?" I don't know... I can't answer that question. I guess I will fall on back in school as I look down at my watch. If I walk a little faster, I will make it to my boring English class. I will ask Lil John, the smartest boy in class, how to spell value and what it means.

I walk back in the building, and the principal, Mr. Dordoo is lusting after one of the new student teachers, and he does not see me as I bust back in through the double doors. The doors make such a loud racket I was sure he would see me. He is too busy gazing at the student teacher's boobs. What an old pervert! Men are something else, and he 'pose to be a preacher, married and has five children.

I walk in the next to the last class of the day and my boring teacher, Ms. Gotmine is standing in the front of the room with a stack of papers. She is dressed in a too loose skirt, and a brown top with some black shoes with wedge wooden heels. She will read for 30 minutes and for 15 minutes she will ask questions. I am sitting right next to Lil John; he smiles as I plop in my chair. His braces cover his buckteeth and the coca cola thick magnifying glasses cover his slim face. I whisper to him, "How do you spell value, and what it mean?" He looks at me with that goofy smile. He said, "Value is spelled, v-a-l-u-e. It means to consider with respect, to be of importance or worth. You got any more words you would like for me to spell or define?

I know a lot of words. Give me some more, please." I said, "That's all the words I have for right now. Thank you!"

Wow, do I think I am important or do I have worth? I don't think that way when I am following in behind some male. I am going to try to do better. Maybe I will follow behind only one boy, well... maybe two. I am too fine to just let all this be enjoyed by only one boy. Haaaa, haaaa! The teacher glances at me for one second and says, "Class, settle down and listen to me." Boy, what a boring, no fun or exciting excuse for trying to teach. Look at her, just here for a paycheck. Man, how many times has she told us I got mine, and you better get yours. How can anybody that's struggling with English learn from the likes of her? Reading subjects of no interest, and asking questions that I did not hear because I don't want to see you or hear your funny, long neck squeaky voice.

Out of frustration I asked, "Can you ever come to class and teach? You read to us er' day. Is this kindergarten? We need for you to make the class fun! Can you do something other than read for 30 minutes and ask questions for 15 minutes? This is the boringness doggone class." The students get completely quiet; most of them are holding their breath and waiting for her to answer. Ms. Gotmine's face turns maroon; she is too dark for her face to turn a different color. She goes over to the door, slowly shuts it and says, in a loud strained voice, "Look, Miss Fast A Hole."

Suddenly, the loudspeaker blurts out, "Ms. Gotmine, the Instructional Area Facilitator is here to evaluate you. This is the principal, Mr. Dordoo; we have been watching and listening to your classroom since the start of the fifth period. Please proceed to the office and bring your personal effects.

"Mane that what's up! How you like me now?" My bore of a teacher glares at me and I glare back with a wink and a smile. As she shuffles papers, grabbing her tan canvas bag full of a disarray of papers and snatching her purse from the bottom drawer with a swift motion, she stumbles as she walks gaped-legged on the tile missing in the floor. She balances her legs and hurries, swinging the door open then slamming it shut with a loud whap.

The class erupts in a thundering roar, legs and arms flailing everywhere. Students are hanging out of the chairs and tears are dropping on desks, clothes and the floor. One shy boy in the back of the room shouts out, "You think she will come back and ask us some more questions?" The laughter is louder and so out of control; several outrageous comments are being made to keep the laughter going. Questions were asked, but not by our teacher. Classmates were asking funny questions about what happened in class today. The bell rang and some of students filed out of class, a girl states, "Wow, first time the class had fun; too bad we had to have fun without Ms. Gotmine."

11

I asked myself, How do you feel about what happened to the teacher? My response: I don't give a damn! She had already called me out of my name when she closed that door, she was 'bout to talk about me bad. She was a lousy teacher and good riddance to her. Lil John, the brainy guy, moves his chair closer and leans his right shoulder into me and says, "How did you have the courage to say that to the teacher? I could never have been brave enough to articulate her academic frailties."

"Why are you always talking funny? Can't you ever talk right?"

Lil John looks funny, wondering what I am talking about. He says, "See you later," as the bell rings. The class noisily dismisses, laughing and talking about the incident; he rounds the corner of the hallway slowly walking out of the class. I watch him walking away, wearing a black long sleeve shirt, high water tight starched jeans that make the swishing sound as he walks down the hall.

I see Miss Goody-Goody Mabel, my sister. She approaches, speaking in her pretend voice, sounding like she got a cold. "What ups, Lil sis?"

"I told you I ain't no kin to you, with your fake self. Why you got to act like you someone you ain't?"

Mabel asks, "Why are you always frustrated, and have to converse with me with verbal aggression? I am your sibling and I adore you."

"Shut up, cow, always changing your voice and talking proper and speaking with all your fancy words. You wanna be a big shot, but you are not just fake. You are a phony. Why can't you be yourself?"

"I want to make something out myself; I dream of a better life. Lou, why are you such a dream killer?"

Ms. Wanna Be More Than She Is runs down the hall crying. I am glad she's gone, always talking and trying to be better than everyone else, flat ass stinky self. I'm glad she crying, Ms. All A's, long dress wearing, thank she's cute with her old looking short alfro wearing self. Ooooh, she gets on my *last* nerve.

~~~~~~

Wrankle up, hard-looking hand touching on me, other wrankle old hand is covering my mouth. I am afraid to talk, but I say, "Leave me alone." I scream quietly as I find myself scrambling, getting up from a kneeling position.

I look around as I walk out of school with a bunch of cheerleaders. For a fleeting moment, I think I might want to join the squad one day. Wow, I can't believe the so-called dream killer got a future dream. I laugh out loud and say to myself, "No way. You so stupid."

I walk slowly down past the school and through the parking lot full of teachers; staff and some of the well to do stuck up students with cars. I walk toward the narrow alley and I see my older brother, Sammie Lee who is always drinking with a balled up, small, brown paper bag in his hand with a gold top peeking out. He's sitting on a wooden crate right near a gray metal trashcan. Every time he sees me, his words are the same, "Sis, let me hold a few dollars." I just want to see him one time sober, and without odor coming from with his body and his stanky clothes.

Have you ever been so shame of your kinfolks? I know I am not perfect, but Sammie Lee ought to be shame. He always says, "Ain't no shame in my game." He so doggone corrupt! His main hustle is always trying to steal, beat someone out of their money or valuables. He dropped out of school and has never held down a job for more than two paychecks. I try to get him to walk me home. He tells me, "I will holler at you, I got some business to take care of. What you can do for me, Lil sis, is go across the street and stall the cashier as I slip some loot under my shirt. If you can't do that, just move it on, Lil sis." I just want to take that bottle and smash it over his dumb ass head. I walk away and just shake my head as I glance over my shoulder. I think to myself, what a drunkard! How can we be related? I think to myself, am I gon' be like him? Will I hold down a job and try to be respectable, or will I try to get my hustle on? Well I gots to think about that; I don't know if I want to be working on these white folks' job.

My grandmomma is old; her skin looks like stale chocolate candy that's been in the package too long. Her hair is long, straw-like silver that is thick and quite wooly. Her once brown eyes have turned dull gray. I know your hair turns gray on your head and all over your body, but I did not know your eye color switches from brown to gray. The eyes are sad and lost. It is a lost that needs to wander off and never be found again. My grandmomma didn't go many places: church, drug store,

13

health clinic, and once a month, grocery shopping.

Grandmomma got married to my grandpa when she was 16 years old, and he was 26 years old. They never hugged, kissed or showed any affection in front of us or in public. She fixed his plate, ran his bath water, scratched his head, washed his clothes and starched his pants and shirts with Niagara starch that was in the red box. She always had money tied to her thigh high stocking.

Late one evening, my grandmomma had a talk with me. Half the time, I didn't know what she was saying. She dropped out in the middle of the sixth grade. She said parts of words, and left some syllables out completely. She could not read or write but she knew several chapters of the Bible by memory. She was a wise woman who had a heart of gold and she was able to foretell the future. She would dream and whatever she told you, it would come true. I don't know how to explain it, but seems like she talked to God and he spoke back to her. She did not want people saying she was a fortuneteller. It's been like she'd pick and choose who she told what was in their future. People were scared of her but at the same time they respected her.

Grandmomma said, "Com." This is how her conversation went. "Lou, come on sot dow rit sid me. I had not sun ya sin yesdidy. Wada ya ben dewing?"

"I been ok," I said.

"Hada ya fas tale runging roun wit thum manash har heada boys? Ya beta bees a christa gal, usa heada me?" I sit near her, straining to understand what is said. Finally I say, "Yes, ma'am." Mabel comes out the kitchen with a too-large-for-her ruffled apron. "The ease of the conversation always amazes me when Mable talks to grandmomma. She does not seem to strain to figure out what she's saying. It was like a foreign language spoken and both of them spoke the same language. I feel like an outsider, a stranger in another land. Mabel and I have not always been close, but this close relationship with Grandmomma seems to split us further apart.

Chapter Two

As Mabel and I got older she seemed to read more books and instead of playing games and hanging out, she started going to the library and finding other folks outside our family to associate with. She was invited to parties and sleepovers that did not include me. I was asked sometimes to join them, but they always talked about stuff I didn't understand. I didn't feel comfortable talking and half the time, I didn't know what to say. When I tried to join the conversation, my statements were always off the subject, and no one would say anything for a while. Mabel said I was trying too hard and I just needed to be myself, when I complained to her. I just decided her and her so-called friends were not my cup of tea, so I did not want to be bothered with those academic snobs.

Now who I *could* relate to was Sammie Lee. He talked my kinda talk. You could talk with him and his friends all day long and not feel out of place. Cussing and talking about stealing and bussing some fool across the head after you pull his or her shirt over their heads. Mane, we used to have some fun. Sammie would have kids to pay him when they walked on the sidewalk near him. He used to say, "Pay the toll booth man," and he was getting paid before and after school. This was my kinda folks they kept it real. I see why Sammie Lee could not stand the ground Mabel stood on. He said, "She act like she too good to be around us." He always talked about her bad. Sometimes, he talked about her and I would feel sorry for her.

Lately, I did not want him to let up on her flat behind. Mane, she needed some weight in her ass. I wondered if she really was our sister for real. Maybe her real momma left her country, alfro-wearing self on our doorstep or she was the neighbor's child. I laugh ever time she walks away; Sammie Lee called her pancake booty, that was the only time she would get mad. I could tell when Mabel was mad. She would frown up and the vein in her forehead would pop out. Without fail, she would call me balloon butt, and she thought that would make me mad. What she did not know is I love my juicy big booty. Big butts ran in the family; I don't know where her long flat behind came from. I always wondered who her kinfolks was. Po' Mabel, she just did not fit or feel comfortable with her own family.

I walk in the doctor's office. On the metal door te words are painted in black, Doctor Wayne Chu. I am breathing hard, out of breathe just thinking about knocking the hell out of those three raunchy hoes.

The young male Asian doctor with straight black low cut hair looked at me and asked me,

"Sit down and tell him my story " "What you mean? Tell you what doggone story?"

"What has happened in your life that has made you angry and so bitter?"

"What are you talking about?" I am not angry or bitter. "Now you about to make me angry, and bitter." Looking at me like you think you know me. "You don't know nothing about me, nothing about me". My voice gets louder and I seem to be getting hot, and anger seems to be building. The doctor looks at me and says in a quiet voice. "Are you angry now?" I want to scream and cuss, but I want to prove him wrong. "No, I am not angry! What makes you ask me that?"

"Louvenia, your voice is elevated, your eyes are dilated, and the vein in your forehead is protruding out. Your fist is closed tight. What happens to make this kind of rage begin? Why?" Can you, Mr. Doctor, make it stop happening? You got some words to tell me that will stop it from happening? I push the paper around his neat little desk. Mane, you got some pills to give this sister that will make me turn into a perfect person? Then you can stick your chest out and say, "I helped this po' black gal." If you can do that you will be called a good doctor. A doctor that be saving all kind of black folks and making them all like you think they oughta be. You will try to make me close to how you behave, but just a little bit beneath you. You don't want to change black folks to be too good. I and my people might get too good and take your little job and be your boss. I will be asking the questions, all proper and using the fancy words, "What your story, Chu?" Pretending like I care, and thangs. Give me a freaking break!

"Louvenia, you are in jail on multiple charges, you have deep-seated anger problems, and you need to identify what is the cause of why you are unable to cope and make the correct decisions. I can help you. I care about helping you make a transformation, but you have to be willing to let me help you. It is your decision; if you don't want my help, please don't waste my time.

I can see another individual. You have exactly sixty seconds to make up your mind."

"Mane, I don't need your help." "You want to get out of jail; I am your ticket. You have forty seconds." "Only person that can help me is a lawyer. You ain't no lawyer; I need a lawyer, not no doc." "You have twenty seconds." I think, I am alone with all my secrets, and he's right about all my anger. What is wrong with me? I am broke, and addicted to drugs, alcohol, sex, and I am a dumb thief.

"Lord," I say out loud, "help me!"

"You have five seconds," he says as he walks over and opens the metal door and turns to the side.

I say, "Ok," in a faint voice. Dr. Chu says in a loud voice, "What did you say?" I shout, "Ok, OK, OK, OK, OK! I need help. Can you please help me, please?"

Head down, no tears, just relieved, chains, heavy stones, seem to be dropping off my shoulders. I slowly breathe out and for the first time in my life, I feel like someone has wrapped their arms around me and is rocking me like a baby. I have the urge to suck my two fingers. The room seems suddenly lighter and I am so calm, I felt like I am high. I feel warmth that no heater or touch could provide. My eyes are closed and I never ever want to open my eyes to this old drab office again. I wonder if heaven will be like this. I feel weightless, so calm, so relaxed, no hunger, no worries just a beautiful feeling of comfort. I close my eyes tightly, just trying to let this glorious feeling to last forever.

What peace!! Dr. Chu interrupts my peaceful voyage. He looks me in my eyes, and holds my hand and says in a quiet, thick-accented voice that I didn't recognize before, "You ha made the rig decsasion of yous life. Goo! Goo! Thaks sho, thaks sho." Bowing his head twice and guiding me to the door, he tells the guard, "I want to sign hur to nother cell." I walk out of the office a new person, never to be the same again. I say quietly to myself in an unrecognizable voice, Thank you, Lord!

Chapter Three

School is in session, and everybody seems to be happy the summer break is over. Me, I am just glad this is my junior year. People are walking around with new clothes and new book bags. Well, they all make me sick; I have on hand-me-down clothes from people I don't know and clothes from my sister Mabel.

"Hey, Lou, my old dress fits you a little tight; why didn't you wear the black dress? It fits loose on me, maybe it will not fit so tight on you."

"Look Mabel, I like my clothes to fit me tight, to show off all these fine curves, my big legs, and this plumb backside you don't know nothing about."

"I just thought the other dress would be more appropriate attire for you to focus on your academic pursuit for this brand new school year." "Well, Miss Thank You So Smart, this time you thought wrong; I wear what I want and do what I want. I don't know why you all up in my business anyway. Move on along. You know I don't fool with your fake ass."

"Why do you always have to have a mean spirit? I was just trying to give you some advice. Why can't you be nice to me sometime, and talk to me like we are family?" "Family? You do not act like anybody in our family. Besides, you don't look like anybody I know in the family. Your hair is so short and kinky, and you are so skinny. Ummm, I just don't know if you are family."

Mabel's eyes started welling up with tears. "Whatever you say, I am your sister. I love you in spite of how hateful you speak to me or act toward me.

She comes close to me and tries to hug me. I look at her and say in a loud voice, "Gon' gal, you ain't no kin to me. Scat." Mabel walks away swiftly, head bowed and shoulders dropped, walking toward the restroom. I thought, She is sad; maybe I ought to go and say, "Sorry." Wow, what's wrong with me? What a dumb thought! I laugh out loud. Mabel turns around right before entering the restroom doors, with tear-filled eyes. I laugh even louder, as she looks and walks in the restroom with that pencil sharp figure. She stomps as she enters the piss room. I laugh even louder as the picture of her continues to flash in my head. I am so overcome with joy and hardcore laughing that tears drop down my face. I gotta use the bathroom and I dare not go in the restroom with her. I gotta use it bad. Maybe I will stop laughing and quietly sneak up behind her and scare the hell out of my so-called sister. I walk toward the restroom on my tiptoes. I hear between sobs Mabel and some strange girl talking.

"Wow, Mabel, I heard your sister talking so bad to you. If that's your sister, I would hate to see your enemy, *Girl!"*

"I have tried so hard to love her. I do not feel love from anyone in my family, except for my grandmother. I am so different from the rest of my family. I don't act, think, eat, or talk like any of them. Believe me, each one of them has told me numerous times that I don't act like anyone in the clan. I am a good person and I do not deserve this kind of treatment I receive from them. I have asked God to help me to love them in spite of the mistreatment. Do you know what God says back to me? 'Love unconditionally.' I just can't take the verbal aggression; it seems to escalate every day. One thing I do know, I have a scholarship to go to a local college, but I will be sending applications to schools miles away and maybe distance from my family will make them realize I am worthy to be loved and respected. I am sorry to be rambling on, but I have no one to talk to about this matter. Thank you for listening and not commenting."

I slowly back up and walk, down the hall. Why she 'gotta be telling our family business? She always using fancy words, it is her fault we can't stand her She 'oughta talk and act like folks.

I had eaten lunch and the school day was almost ending and I was happy. Why did I feel so good? Oh, I forgot, my last two boring classes are in the same room. The students did not switch classes. The teacher moved from class to class during the fifth and sixth periods. This is going to be some good sleep. I prop my feet on one chair and lean down in a second chair in the back of the dusty classroom. There is an old bookcase with ragged books stuffed randomly on the shelf. Old wrinkled up papers and manila folders were tossed every which way. The last thing I heard before going to dream world was, "Let her dumb ass sleep, she don't know nothing anyway. I got mine, and she will not get hers. I predict she will be a mother with a house full of bad children."

I think to myself, She better be glad I am sleepy, because I will tell that cow about her ugly, wig-wearing, too much light makeup, no-shape-havin' self.

I was walking from school my sophomore year, and I went to the store to pick up a snack. I walked out drinking a red soda and eating a honey bun. Two pale cops blocked the alley where I was about to approach. One short cop got out, slapping the car door as loud as he could, tossing his cap in the front seat. He looked at me and said, "I got a report you stole an item from the store back there. Ms. Chu said you paid for the drink, but you put that honey bun in those tight ass faded blue jeans that are showing your curves and put a package of gum in those sweet looking bosoms of yours." He moves closer and the tall lanky younger cop gets out the passenger side of the car, walking very slow, eyes and another area bulging to the max. The two of them walk closer as I move toward the wooden white-framed building. I show no fear as I continue to swallow the drink held in my right hand and eat the honey bun in my left hand.

The two cops don't have a gun or a stick and I am going to take care of some good old-fashioned ass whupping business. I am gon' toss the drink at the short one, throw the honey bun in his eyes, and for the tall one I am going for the low jewel sticking out, ready to be kicked over and over again. As I plan to take action, another policeman comes up. He says, "What do we have here?" The cops begin to ramble, looking startled. The lieutenant walks up and in a calm voice say, "You officers return to the squad car; I will deal with you two later." I have told you two about this over and over again. The cops walk to the car, get in and drive away. The short gray-haired man moves slowly towards me and says, "I apologize for the officers' behaviors. I can see why they are lusting after you. You are fine. If I were straight, I would not mind getting a piece." "Do you have any brothers that are as fine as you?" I say nothing as I switch my big rump past this freak.

~~~~~~

The last class bell rings as I wake up from my exciting slumber, smiling. The eleventh grade teacher hollers out as I stretch my legs and spring up from the chair.

"You need to go to sleep at night, and stop sleeping in school. I thought about waking you up, but I changed my mind; I said it was just a waste of time."

"Well you know I was sleep in the first hour of Mrs. Thomas' boring class. I woke up for the first part of your class and saw you reading from your notes the exact same information that's in the book and could not take two stale, boring teachers, so I rather sleep and dream about something exciting and adventurous."

She's mad at my comments, and tries to block the door with a small ruler in her hand as I get up to leave after hearing the last bell of the school day."Ma'am, you don't want to try nothing with me at the end of the school day. I know where your little yellow beetle car is parked. It is down the side street a block from the school. I saw when you parked the car this morning and put the emergency brake on because the car is on a slight hill. You don't want none of this. Somebody better school this fake educator before she is car-less. Same time, same place tomorrow. See ya player." One of my classmates catches up with me and says, "Girl, you ain't got no sense. She may get you suspended first thing in the morning." "No, I don't think so; I saw what she was doing in her car, don't play. She will not be suspending me, that's on the real." "Tell me, wha wha did ya see?" "MYOB, get ya some business! I will check you later. Be breezee!!!"

The next day after school I am walking down the hall and look up and see in big, bold, colorful, magic marker letters on white freezer paper a poster stating, Cheerleader Tryouts Today Right After School In The Gym! I walk around the corner to the left and then another right and I see a line of girls signing a yellow lined paper. I find myself standing in the crooked line, signing my name and my grade classification with a yellow number #2 pencil. I see most of the well-to-do girls with their slender figures in that line. I am standing near a female not much bigger than the pencil I just put back on the wooden clipboard. On the other side of me is a girl bigger than me. She has about twenty-five more pounds on me. We are the meat among all these bones; our eyes meet and we have an instant bond. We know as we both survey the crowd that we are the first two that will be on the cut list. The school is known for selecting high yellow girls whose parents are the Who's Who in the community. Well, I am determined to be a cheerleader and my new friend will also be a member on the squad with me. We have two things in common: poundage and being born to poor parents. I extend my hand toward her and say, "Hi, my name is Louvenia; we are the finest thangs in the crowd."

"Yes, I agree. My name is Angel." Angel is a pretty, dark chocolate with the prettiest white pearl teeth. She has a smile that brightens up the room. The others girls are in sets of three conversing with each

21

other. The groups glance over at the two of us, holding their mouths and squeezing their eyes, laughing with a quiet, dignified laughter. I look at the three groups and say in my most proper voice, "I hope ya make the squad, 'cause, Lou and Angel sho' will be picking out our uniform."

"I hear someone faintly say, 'This is not the sign up for the Stout Girls' Eating Class.' Angel shouts, "Who you callin' stout?" "My name is Angel, for your information." I steps two steps in front of Angel and says to her, "I gots this in my ghetto language. "Yawl musta didn't hear me when I said, "My name is *Louveeenya*. If ya been around this school at least one year, you fousa know me. If ya know me, you know I kick asses and take names. Don't even try to step here." The tall slender attractive lady in a blue jogging outfit with shoulder length hair quickly walks up to the sign-in sheet, asking in a sweet calming voice, "Has everyone signed up for two weeks of rigorous cheerleading tryouts?" No one said a word; we all was looking at this tall beautiful lady that walked in with such style and urgency. Instant girl crush, not in a sexual way, but admiring one female to the utmost. Wow! This is our teacher/sponsor/coach! She breaks the room trance, asking again, "Did everyone sign this sheet?" All heads bounce up and down. No utterance of words being vocalized. "I am Mrs. McClanahan. I asked a question and I am used to hearing responses. Did everyone sign this sheet?" She dangles the yellow paper, waving it rapidly in the air. The echo of, "Yes, ma'am" circles the gym with a pretty rhythmic sound.

"Thank you! Everyone gather over here; I have some permission slips that your parents must sign before we begin the tryouts. If you are interested in becoming a Tiger cheerleader, conduct must be satisfactory, grades of "C" or higher, punctuality and attendance must be satisfactory. Everyone who makes the squad must be able to purchase the uniform. You must be able to perform twenty-five dance movements and be able to run three miles in at least 40 minutes. You will need a comfortable shirt, shorts and a pair of tennis shoes. Tryouts will last ten days, and after the end of the tenth day, 15 out of these 25 people will be selected. See you after school on Monday. Oh and ladies, you may want to work out this weekend; you have a long, hard week ahead of you. Good luck to each one of you."

Chapter Four

It is Monday after school, thirty minutes into the tryouts and I am bent over with my palms on my knees, and I am exhausted and wanting to give up and forget about this waste-of-time tryout.

I look over at Angel and she is not sweating or showing any signs of fatigue. How is that possible? She is in shape and I am over here about to pass out. The football team comes in to run the bleachers. I look over and watch the finest males running single file from the top to the bottom of the bleachers and back again, over and over. Coach Johnson blows his black whistle and shouts, "Run faster!" I gaze at the firm bodies and instantly I get a burst of energy. I am moving with vigor, and I mean with unbelievable vigor. The routine is imprinted in my head and fast rhythmic steps are executed with such precision. I smile and I know I am standing out among the other girls. The pivots, turns, jumps, extensions of my extremities are extraordinary. I see all eyes are on me. The other girls are breathing hard and the repeated drills are met with grumblings and signings; I, on the other hand, am excited and thrilled to continue the routine without a complaint.

I spin around and complete three somersaults, finishing with a cool split and land right in front of the fine football player, Martavious. He was bending down with one foot in the air when he became off balance, tying up his big ass shoes. He tumbled and his face falls in my lap. Wow! This muscular, chocolate, low-cut hair dude, with a small sexy gap in his pearly white teeth, glaring up at me as we both are laid out on the floor. I smile as I erupt into a loud laugh. He laughs, and everyone in the gym begins laughing with a loud roar. They called this handsome stud, Big Tae. His broad shoulders wiggle back and muscular biceps bulk up as he clumsily stands his bowlegs to attention. His large hand extends to me, as I am still on the floor; the view is breathtaking. I slowly grab his hand and try and open my mouth to say something clever. Both the football coach and the cheerleader sponsor shout together, "Get back to practice!"

My teacher screams at me, "I can't believe you still don't know how to spell your name. Your Mammy should have named your stupid butt a name that would not take you forever to learn. Practice, girl! Practice! Practice!"

23

I walk over to the squad, and everyone is looking past me. I hear footsteps and as I turn, I see Big Tae walking towards me with my blue washcloth nestled in his hand. He extends his hand to return it to me and I can really use it to wipe the dripping sweat that seems to be pouring from all the pores on my body. He gives the washcloth to me and jerks it back quickly. He passes it to me kissing my hand softly with his chocolate, thin, bulging lips. The air seems one hundred degrees hotter! Wheee!

"My name is Martavious Robinson and I am sorry for the collision. Well, I am not sorry. Can I walk you home after this?"

"I don't know you; you might be a bad guy out to hurt me." The girls around me look with envy in their eyes. Angel, the other girl that was disliked by the squad said, "I'll walk with y'all if you need a friendly escort." "Hey," Ms. McClanahan shouts, "this is not the dating game; let's move it along. Tae, I think you need to finish running the bleachers before your coach, who appears to have a look of disapproval, brings his wooden paddle over here."

"I didn't catch your name," he says as he walks swiftly backwards. I scream out with a smile on my face, "I did not throw it."

Two hours later, I walk out the locker room and who do I see as I take two steps? Big Tae. I am going to play it cool for once in my life. I will try not to be so desperate. Can I pull it off, being cool, pretending not to be interested? I don't know how long I can pretend, because wow, he is soooo fine!

"Hey, excuse me; I need two things from you."

I scream in my head, "Any, anything." My facial expression, says, "Get lost!"

"First, I would like to know the name of the girl I am walking home. Second, do you mind if I walk you home, and where do you live?

"Look, you fall in my lap, and now I am supposed to let you, a stranger, walk me to my house?"

"I would like to respond to you, but I need to know your name. Can you please tell me your name?"

I look with disapproval and blurt out, "Louvenia." Lowering my voice I add, "But everybody calls me Lou."

"Louvenia, will it be all right if I call you Lou?" Big Tae says in a quiet, respectful way.

Gee, I believe I like the way I am handling this situation. I slowly say, stuttering, "I guess you can call me Lou."

"Dog, I am glad I got your permission. Now, can I walk you home?"

"It's a free country," I say rapidly.

"Can you answer my question?"

I better be a little nice. "Yes, you can, Tae."

"What? You remember my name? I am impressed. Can I ask you one more question?"

"Is this some kind of interview?"

"I always interview and question possible girlfriends." I look in his eyes, smiling in my head but on the outside I give him a puzzled look.

"Last question."

I say, "Ask away since you seem to be on a mission."

"Do you find me cute?"

I say, "Cute in a non-committed way."

Tae says, "Let me rephrase the question. Are you attracted to me?"

I can't hold it together, I am tired from tryouts and this fool wants to know if I find him attractive. Perspiration is dripping everywhere! I look him up and down, and blurt out, "I live in Burlington Street Projects."

"I know where that is, I have some first cousins that live on the 200th block." He tries to grab my hand, touching the tips of my fingers. I pull away, grabbing my book bag as it drops to the ground. We both stoop down, knees touching so gently, I almost fall face down on the ground. What a missed opportunity! I quickly remember, Oh, I am playing hard to get. I get up slowly, and we seem to gradually stand up gazing in each other's eyes.

I see Tae catching the game-winning football as he makes the fourth and last touchdown. He's speeding to the end zone, quickly turning and pointing at me as I jump in the air, styling in my tight, short cheerleader outfit. I am dressed in pink at the prom, dancing the night away.

"Hey, Lou! Are you listening to me?"

"What! What! Huhn?"

"I said, do you think you will make the cheerleader squad? Can't you hear?"

"Yes, I can hear, and yes I will make the squad."

"What if you do not make it?"

"I will make it!"

"What's your Plan B if you don't make it?"

"Why? You don't think I will make it?"

"Yes, I believe you will, but sometimes you need to be prepared if your plan is not in line with God's plan. Sometimes God will not let *your* perfect plan work out on your timetable. If you understand that concept, you will not feel like a failure if things do not work out exactly as you planned. You must remember God is in control, your plan may be delayed or a better, Godly plan may be in store for you."

"What, you some kinda preacher?"

"No, I learned that lesson the hard way. I will pray that God gives you the desires of your heart."

"Hey, you will include me in your prayer? I did not know people could pray for small things like getting a spot on a cheering squad."

"You can pray for anything. Do you go to church?"

"I used to go, but I had a bad church experience with a minister."

"I am sorry to hear that. Some ministers make it bad for the good ones."

"My father is a minister and he is not an angel, but he strives to walk with God. As a preacher's kid I have to try and walk the same path. I try to do what the good books says; it is a struggle, but I pray constantly for God to direct my steps."

I like this guy; he is a little too holy compared to the people I normally hang out with. Tae is gentle, and easy to talk with and his conversation is not about getting some and for some strange reason, my mind is not there either.

"This is where I live."

"Oh, I was enjoying myself. I hate we got to your stoop so fast," Tae says in a slow tone.

"Well, I better get in the house before the street lights come on."

"Okay", I better get home too before they turn on."

"Tae turns, looking down at his wristwatch, and shouts, "I'll see you tomorrow."

"Tae," I calmly say, "I find you quite attractive!" My eyes drop down quickly as I turn, running through the open door and down to apartment number three.

Chapter Five

The cheerleader squad was announced on the last day of practice, which was on a Friday. I made the cheerleader squad along with the other unlikely candidate Angel. We were so happy we hugged each other and instantly did two cartwheels and a split, which were the ending steps to one of our favorite routines. Angel and I became close because the other girls didn't want to have anything to do with us. We didn't care, we saw them as invisible and that didn't sit well with them. When we were first introduced as the new squad, Angel and I got a standing ovation during the first prep rally on Monday. Our names were called one by one as we ran in the gym in front of the whole student body. The two of us seemed to get more attention from teachers and students than the other girls. This did not go over well with the other cheerleaders and they tried to make things hard for us. We were so happy to be a part of the squad and most people seemed to enjoy seeing that girls that had meat on their bones were finally allowed to be Hillside cheerleaders. What a joyful moment!

One hour after leaving the library, I am in my room and I ask myself, what is wrong with you? I seem so content, happy, and nice to people, caring and kind. I am even a little nicer to Mabel.

I am changing, but it's something about her; I just can't be too nice to her. She will start to talk to me like we are close and I can't seem to take her voice. I guess I just don't like her looks. She is still so different from how everyone in the family looks. Mabel likes Tae and she tells me, "He is such a positive match for you." I tune her out. I am looking at her and watching her lips move, but I don't hear anything she is saying.

I am escorted to my new cell. I pass by the three heifers that I was in the cell with when I was first brought in. They shout out, "I'm glad they moving your big crazy ass in another cell. We already packed your funky ghetto clothes in this paper sack, hoe!" I walk by and do not acknowledge they are even talking.

"What's wrong? Cat got your tongue or did Doc give your crazy behind some happy meds?"

I pass and even though I want to cuss, my legs keep moving and no words are spoken. I just walk in the cell and go straight to sleep.

It's time for chow, which means a single line and no talking, and keep your arms on the sides of your body. I file in line and I see young, middle aged, and very old women. Everyone seems to be sad and hopelessness seems to fill the air. The guards have batons and the men as well as women seem to have no mercy. I feel despair and my eyes fill with tears. The quietness is so crushing that I scream out, "Lord, have mercy!" and fall to the floor. The whole room stops and the guards gather around me, batons ready to strike a blow. My eyes are shut and I hear, "You are going to learn to shut your damn mouth."

"Stop! Put down the batons."

What are you going to do?"

"My God, what kind of staff are you that you would beat a defenseless prisoner without any cause. Tell me, what did she do?" The lady with a white collar around her neck is dressed in a manly black suit. She reaches down and grabs my wrist and stands me up slowly, looking like she is seeing into my soul.

"I have heard from these ladies that this happens, but I have actually witnessed it for myself. I have not gotten an answer for what this brand new prisoner did to have four officers wanting to physically abuse her."

"She became disruptive and let out a violent outburst, disturbing the peace."

"What? She said, and I quote, 'Lord, have mercy!' Making that statement warrants being beaten by two men and two women? These ladies are allowed to talk during mealtime and various types of music are to be played. I will report this incident, and some disciplinary action will be taken; I can assure you of this."

She turns and looks at me. "Ma'am, are you okay?"

"Yes, thank you for asking."

"My name is Minister North and if you have any retribution from this incident, here is my card. Give me a call, if you have any problems." Minister North walks away, and as soon as she is out of sight, the tall male guard with the wrinkled up, grease-stained uniform snatches ups the card. He glares at me with spit on his big chapped lips and snot coming from his big bumpy nose and says in a low voice, "You better not never tell her anything about what's going on around here. You better say this incident never happened, if you know what's good for you."

I walk over to get my tray and while in line I hear the music come on and at the same time my former cell mate tells me I got everybody in trouble and I will pay dearly. I close my eyes quickly and pray. I guess it's not *how* you pray, but *when*!

~~~~~~

The library is closing, and the lights have blinked on and off; the signal to get your stuff and exit the building. As we stroll down the sidewalk leaving the library, Tae asks me again about church. Tae has asked me to come to his church this Sunday, and I have run out of excuses. I've told him I don't have any money, nice clothes or shoes. I even said, "My momma may not let me." He told me I don't need any money, and I can wear any kind of clothes or shoes.

He asks me if he can speak to my mother. "I have wanted to meet her since you will be meeting my dad and mom after church Sunday."

"Hey, Tae, you are taking this way too fast. I have not agreed to go to church and you got me meeting your parents. What's the deal?"

"I told them I was bringing my girlfriend to church."

I took in a gulp of air and softly said, "I am not your girlfriend, buddy."

"Who is buddy? I am Tae," he says, smiling with a short fake laugh.

"Tae, this is not funny. I don't mind you making plans to walk me home or even to go to the library, but you seem to leave me out of things you are deciding to do. Am I a doll that you can pull my string and I move and perform as you see fit?"

"Sweetie, I am truly sorry; I do not want to make you angry. First, let me make this right! Lou, do me the honor of being my girlfriend?" I look at him pissed off. He is so chocolate brown gorgeous, I can't be mad long. I don't smile; even though I want to, I don't.

I say, "I don't know, I got to think about it."

He looks puzzled and I say, "I thought about it, yes!" For the first time he grabs my hand, pulls me close and kisses me ever so softly, squeezing my hands.

"Tae, let's get one thing straight; I am not your puppy. You say come, I come. You say sit, I sit. Do you understand?"

"Yes, sweetie."

"For starters, don't call me sweetie anymore. Okay?"

"Okay."

"Maybe I have been a little pushy, but you just don't know how much I really, *really like you!*"

"Now what about meeting your mother, going to church, and meeting my parents?"

"Hold your horses, partner!"

"What horse? Who is partner?"

"You got a lot of jokes! Let's take it slow. Let me get used to being your girlfriend and that kiss you just gave me…"

"What! You didn't like it?"

"I enjoyed it, just slow down. You about to make me faint."

"You can faint! I would like to have an excuse to hold you in my arms again."

"Tae, can I give you an answer to those two questions tomorrow?"

"Yes, my sweetie, sorry, I mean Lou." We walk home in silence. Both of us seem to enjoy swinging our hands and walking and moving in a steady cadence. I walk up my steps and blow a kiss goodbye to my new boyfriend. He grabs it, puts it close to his heart and turns, making his way home.

Chapter Six

I walk in the house and of course my mother is not at home. Mabel has left turnip greens, sliced green tomatoes, a few thin-sliced sweet potatoes, and one cornbread muffin on a plate for me. We never have meat during the week, only on Sunday and it's always smothered chicken or pork chops. The gravy is always so good with those larger-than-life biscuits. Mabel is folding towels and I thank her from the kitchen for saving me a plate that is warm from being on top of the stove. Plastic saran wrap is covering the plate tightly so roaches and flies will not have a feast before I can digest the meal. I eat the food and it is so good.

Mabel has put the other children to bed and is still doing chores at 8:00 p.m. She looks weary as I walk in the small cramped sitting room. She does her best to take care of us since our grandmother is not feeling well. I think to myself, I need to help out a little more around the house. I could tell her I am going to step up and start helping out around here, but she might expect me to do more than I am willing to do.

"Lou, you might want to get your clothes ironed and ready for school tomorrow."

"Okay, let me wash my plate and glass, first."

"What? No attitude, Louvenia?" Mabel asked cautiously. "I just knew you were going to say"—marking my voice—"'Shut up talking to me; you are not my mother. You are no kin to me. Say one more thing to me and I promise, I will knock the taste out of your mouth.'"

"First, I do not sound like that, and I have a new boyfriend, Tae, and I am trying to be a better person." Wow! My prayers have been answered; she rushes over to hug me and I extend my hand. She grabs it, moves it aside and hugs me anyway.

Suddenly, the lock jiggles and the door opens wide. Mama is high and she slurs, "You heifers funny now? What's up in here? Lou you always acting like you can't stand Mabel and now you all hugged up looking like you 'bout to kiss."

"Mama what are you saying?" Mabel asks, raising her voice. I look at Mama in disbelief.

"Look, hussies; Mabel with your flat butt, and Lou with your double butt, y'all better remember who is grown in this house. It is not the likes of you two quenches, I am the damn Mammy and don't you ever forget

31

it," voice elevating with each word. As she looks around the room she screams out, "Who moved the furniture around and made this room look so crowded?"

Mabel confesses in a lower tone than she used before, stating, "I did. I thought the change would give the room a nice English charm."

"What? You on that dope? I see why no one can't stand your high for looting black ass," screaming to the top of her voice.

"Momma, keep your voice down. You are going to wake up the neighbors!"

"Gal, fu—"

Before she could curse, we notice Grandmomma standing in the hallway resting her frail body, bending forward over the silver walker. "I knows you been drinking, but that loud bad talking is going to stop rat now. God don't like ugly. Bedtime ever' body. Y'all need to go to sleep."

"Look, I am grown and Ma, I am not ready to do nothing unless I want to do it."

Mabel and I start to move toward our room; we do not need to witness the throw down that is about to erupt.

Chapter Seven

~~~~~~

I am eight years old and I have stopped playing in the closet. I don't feel safe in there.

It is Sunday and my grandfather is the pastor of a small congregation, mostly family folks.

He drinks and gets drunk right after he preaches his sermon. He is always trying to hug me, and the women in the family are always pulling me from his tight embrace. They never say a word to my grandfather or me, they just usher me away from him.

One Sunday night, it's quite late and I should have been in the bed hours ago. I am playing my favorite board game, Mouse Trap. I am in the corner behind the Queen Ann blue chair. Someone could walk by me and never see me; this is my new hiding place. The house is completely quiet; the silence is broken by loud sounding footsteps. The sound stops close to my hiding spot and I hold myself completely still. No sound is heard for a few seconds and the walking continues down the hall until I no longer hear the walking. I continue playing and having a good time with the game. Bam! Grandfather is on the floor next to me *very close*. He is rubbing on me and tugging on my jeans. Just when I am about to say, "No," he places his big rock heavy hands over my mouth and his other hand is tugging at my jeans. A flash of bronze feet appears at the foot of the chair. My grandfather with his drunken stinky self jumps to his feet. He stands face to face with my grandmomma. He starts saying, "The mouse tray was not working and Lou wanted me to fix it."

"You sa was sa fix em wit your sa hand on hut mouth and hus pants?" Grandmomma quickly extends her two fingers making a v sign and saying these words very loudly and in a strange voice. "You shall die, and not live, because you do not declare the works of the Lord!"

Monday morning at noon he was dead. He was found at the foot of the stairs. He had bruises in the middle of his back. The coroner said the marks resembled bruises of a victim that had been pushed. Grandfather had bruises all over him so that was not enough proof that he was pushed.

I will not forget the last time I saw grandfather alive. I remember

33

how Grandmomma held her two fingers out and said those unforgettable words. People heard what happened and they said she put a hex on him. Other folks said she poisoned his food. Grandmomma did not ever tell me to stop talking about the incident nor did she ever care what other people were saying.

She never said a word. Two weeks later my grandfather was funeralized; preachers and relatives from up north and folks from all over Shelby County were there. Not a single soul cried except for Sammie Lee, and some young woman with two small children that favored everyone in our family. The woman held her children close and softly cried throughout the whole service. People were whispering and I was trying to eavesdrop, but I could not understand what they were saying about the woman and her children. I asked Grandmomma, "Who is that lady?" She replied,

"That is not a lady." I was totally confused and the look on her face was one of disappointment and anger.

During the repast, it was like a big happy party. Singing and dancing and a lot of back door whispering. I was certainly one of the people filled with joy, along with all the female kinfolks. Sammie Lee was sad because his teacher who taught him to drink and the art of chasing women was gone. I believe the only reason he was grieving was his classes were ended abruptly and he would never be able to finish the multiple lessons taught by the greatest married player of all time, in Sammie's opinion.

Sammie Lee said, "Grandfather's death was not an accident. Grandfather could drink all day and still walk a straight line. He could drop to the floor and pick up a dime and in an instant, he could stand straight up and not waver or wobble after drinking two fifths of whiskey. I know the man did not fall, and the police report indicated he had bruises in his back. I bet you any kind of money he was pushed from the back." One unknown cousin told him to stop talking. His voice got even louder. He shouted, "Nobody can make me shut up. I wish someone would try." A hush came over the room. Sammie Lee turned his right shoulder and as he saw Grandmomma, a fearful look came over Sammie Lee's face. She walked up to the serving line and got a plate and filled it with food. She came and sat right next to Sammie Lee. He and all the family ate in total silence.

A week after my grandfather's funeral, I began thinking about how

34

a so-called preacher could do the same kind of things men in the street do. He stood up every Wednesday and Sunday and talked about being a servant of God and outside the church he was no different from the homeless man that lives in a box, drunk in the alley. He touched me in places he was not supposed to and no one said, "Stop." I was the only one that said those words and he stopped me by covering my mouth. I vowed that day I would never trust a preacher again. I never wanted to talk to or be around one ever again. I was in the bed, and it was late and I cried myself to sleep.

Chapter Eight

I believe I am the most hated person in the prison. The other inmates do not want to be near me and the guards talk to me with such disgust. I feel slightly lonely. No one comes to see me during visitation and I have no one to talk to except my psych doctor. I have not attempted to call anyone during phone time; I can't bear to tell my family I am again in jail. I can't bear to see the disappointing and judgmental looks of disapproval. The family is always scraping up dollars trying to keep me out of jail. When they gather their hard earned money, especially Mabel, I never say thank you or listen to them when they give me some advice. I have been ungrateful, and acted like my family should help me because I am related to them. I feel ashamed, embarrassed and I can't, and will not let them go through the mess I've made again. I drop my head and cover my face with ten fingers engulfing my face. I am in the chow hall and I am not hungry. In the last few days I have not been eating. My bright orange jumpsuit starts to sag.

"Well, well, Ms. Big Butt, you too good to eat this food?" As she begins to talk, other women gather around me and in a quick second I am in the center. Two big women stand with their backs to me blocking any view of me, and this skinny-legged, tall, beanpole, freckled, red-dye haired skank says, "I didn't tell you my name; it is kick-ass Tasha. I have not whupped a big ass in a while and it's time for me to get some practice in. Thanks to you I can get my practice in with my favorite song playing. I can beat you till I get tired since the guards hate your guts." She grabs me by my hair and slings me on the ground as she and several heifers take turns kicking me.

My foot is kicking Ms. Ophelia after I grab a handful of her hair. I am angry because she tried to break up the fight between her child and mine. I am smiling as I kick her over and over. "Get off, get off her, please!"

No one is shouting, "Get off her!" even when my nose starts to bleed and the pain is so unbearable. I think back to Ms. Ophelia and all the people Lou and all my children jumped on for the fun of it. I can barely keep my eyes open as I crunch, holding my head as the kicking continues. I don't make a sound, but the screaming in my head is so loud I am about to touch the stars that hang inches from my face. I don't know how I can make them stop. I scream out,

"Forgive these ladies, Lord." I wonder what inmate said those words and instantly the kicking stops. I double over and hold myself, wrapping myself in the fetal position, rocking myself from side-to-side, from left to right. The group scatters and I am in the middle of the floor, groaning softly like a wounded animal. As I look up all eyes are on me, a few have tears in their eyes. I had planned to take the hits and not make a sound.

I am moaning, but I realize that it was me that cried out to forgive these ladies that were attacking me. I can't believe in the middle of an attack I asked God to forgive them. Right now as I think about this abuse, I do not call these people out of their names; I call them ladies. I am losing my mind. I am hurting; pain is coming from all areas of my body. What is wrong with me? I need help. I can't believe I am not devising a plan to get all that were involved.

An old dark hand grabs my hand and she kneels beside me. Tasha shouts, "Leave her alone before you get the same, Granny Mo." "Do what you do, but enough is enough! Guards, you need to do your jobs." One of the men came over and said, "Was a fight going on? What happened? Do we have any witnesses?" "Please stop with the fake concern," the older woman said with an angry tone. "Leave her alone." "Everybody, it's time to go back to your cell," the guards shout out. As the inmates are walking single file to the cell, the male guard whispers, "That's what you get, hussy. Next time, I will not let the beating stop until they kill you and we have to tote you out of here in a body bag, whore!"

I walk unsteadily and wonder if I will ever get out of here alive. No one knows I am in this place. I may have to rethink not calling my family. I am hurting and for the first time in my life, I can't fight my own battles. I am out numbered and I must surrender my life over to a higher power. I have no one to count on. Lord help me! I have no one to count on.

Chapter Nine

Tae wants me to go to church with him and he wants to talk to my mother or grandmomma about my church visit. He wants to get permission for me to go to church and have Sunday dinner with his family, the Robinsons. I am not sure I want to go to church or even meet his preacher father. Tae is walking me home from school and Grandmomma is on the porch with her flowered, zip-up housecoat dress. He walks straight up to her and introduces himself. He informs her we are dating and he would like for me to go to his church on Sunday and after church have dinner at his home. He tells her that after dinner he will make sure I come straight back home.

Grandmomma looks at him, moves close to him and the only word she says is "Fine." No broken English, no Jamaican dialect can be detected. We walk off a little from the porch and he says to me, "That was not so bad. I thought it was going to be a hard task." I look at him and he seems so content and I am not sure if I am ready to meet his folks. I really like Tae, and I never had a dude that has treated me with this kind of affection. I feel really good, but part of me worries how his family will treat me. My family has lots of problems and his parents are educated and they may not approve of him talking to a girl like me. I tried to voice my concern and he said, "You are my girl and no one will break us up."

It's Saturday night and I have five dresses that cover the bed. I wonder which dress I will wear. It's two a.m. and I am still not sure what I will put on. I need to get in the bed, so I will not be sleep in church. I count sheep, clouds, the numbers backward from 100 and I repeat the alphabet five times. I just cannot seem to fall asleep. When I finally fall asleep, momma comes in the room screaming, waking up Mabel and me. She wants to know why the light is still on, using up the electricity. I tell her I can't seem to fall asleep. She is drunk and she says, "If I beat the hell out of you I bet your ass will go to sleep. She raises her hand and she falls to the floor. She struggles to get up and I try to help her. She pushes me and staggers down the hall. Mabel and I look at each other and we both crawl back in the bed. Mabel is sleep first and her soft snoring is soothing. I breathe in and out, eyes closed and I fall into dreamland.

Tae tells me to be ready by 8:30 a.m. because he wants me to eat breakfast at church before his teen Sunday school. I am ready by 8:00 a.m. and I hope he comes early before my drunken momma wakes up. Mabel helps me pin my hair up in a bun with bobby pins. She says I look cute and I am not as nervous as I thought I would be. A three-knock sound hits on the wooden door.

I am in the sitting room and as soon as I open the door, I rush out holding his hand and walking swiftly down the stairs.

We walk toward a church I have passed many times and never thought to look in the direction of the church. We hold hands as we walk up a long flight of stairs and enter through the open door. When we walk in the vestibule, a lady in all white greets us. She has on a long white dress, white stockings, shoes, and a pair of gloves on her hands. I see several of them and I ask why all the nurses are at the church. He smiles and says they are ushers who seat people who enter, giving out programs that contain the order of service and they are in charge of taking up the money during the offering period.

We walk down the cramped wooden stairs, and get in line for the breakfast that is being served. There are pans of eggs, grits, biscuits with gravy, bacon, sausage, coffee, orange juice and milk. The ladies in aprons are friendly and they serve up a nice hefty portion of food on our plates. We grab two seats in the back and all eyes watch as Tae pulls the chair out for me and as he patiently waits until I sit down. I ask him why he waited to sit down as I clumsily try to figure out what do with my purse. He told me a gentleman always waits until a lady sits down before he does. I stood up when my quarter I was going to put in the offering tray rolled out of my pocket and under the table next to ours. When I got back to the table he was standing up and he did not sit down again until I sat down. All this gentleman stuff was making me feel weird and all the people watch our every move. I was hungry and was about to put food in my mouth, but before I picked up the fork, Tae said a short prayer. I try not to eat my food too fast, considering my every move is being viewed. After drinking the orange juice, I was happy to leave the breakfast table and was glad when Tae said, "Are you ready to go to my Sunday school class?"

We walk down the hall to a class of twelve teen boys and girls. Tae introduces me to the teacher and all the students in the class. Two girls roll their eyes at me when their names are called. I guess they have a crush on him and they probably wonder what he sees in me. I smile and laugh to myself when he pulls the chair out from the conference table. The class is talking about Moses when he put the staff down and parted the red sea. The teacher asks if the students would be frightened if the sea opened up and raging water several feet above their heads was moving and splashing wildly. The teacher states this was a time when the Hebrew people's faith in God was tested. Most of the class agrees that they would be frightened as they walked the river bottom and they would watch the sides of the water very closely.

Tae discusses his feelings and his faith and he says he would be in constant prayer during their long journey fleeing from the Egyptians soldiers. The hour long class ended and I did not make one comment, because even though I remember the story from the movie, I did not want anyone to know I had not read it in the bible. I was having trouble finding the book of Exodus when Tae went to restroom and the instructor told the class to turn to the chapter. I had no idea of where to look for it in the Bible. Everyone had found the book and the pages were swishing as I was thumbing, looking in the back of the Bible. I glance at one of the guy's Bible and notice that his pages are turned to the very front of the book. I was sweating and after it seemed like it took forever, I found the quoted scripture. I was glad when the class was ending; the prayer requests and long, song-like prayer adjourned the class.

Tae and I walk upstairs and are seated by a bowlegged, gray-haired usher who walks us to the front pew on the left side of the church. The singing of the male chorus is good and I feel really calm. Tae's father, Pastor Robinson stands up and prays, sings a song and gives his sermon title. His three points, and two stories are ok, but I am kinda sleepy so I heard some of the sermon, but during my brief nap I was confused and could not connect all his points to the message title. After the benediction, his father makes his way to the back of the church, greeting the churchgoers. I hear a person say to him that the sermon was inspiring and I say the same but I say, "Pastor, the sermon was inspiring." Tae tells his father, "This is my girlfriend Lou." He looks at me and says, "It's nice to finally meet you." He asks if I will join the family for dinner and I say, "Yes, sir." He tells Tae to go to the car and the family will all meet in five minutes after he locks up his office.

We drive up to their nice brick home and his father pulls the car in the double carport. I touch the knob to get out of the car and instantly Tae is at the door opening it before I step out. He holds my hand and leads me to the door, unlocking it as we walk in, stepping on the shiny hardwood floors. I sit down on the sofa putting my pocketbook on the end table next to the brass lamp. His mother had come home earlier and she came in the living room and introduced herself and told us to come in the dining room because the food was ready. The prayer was said, and the food in the bowls was passed around and everyone was filling their own plate. Small talk was shared and it was a pleasant experience.

Tae's parents invited us to come to the place in their home called a sunroom. The father asked what college I planned to attend, and had I started taking college entrance exams. I said, "No, I am not sure of what exactly I'm going to do. Tae's mother grabbed his hand and said to her son, "Let's clean off the table and wash and dry the dishes. I rose up to go with them and his father told me to stay, he wanted to talk a little more to me. He told me his son seemed to like me very much and he was headed to college and had a promising future and he did not need anything that would keep him from succeeding. He told me he did not want any traps put in his son's path. He had a funny look on his face and said, "You know what I mean, because you've been around." He said, "Tae is so innocent and quite green, and I would hate if something kept him from accepting scholarships to go off to college. I want you to promise that whatever happens you will not hinder him from going to school." Before I could answer, Tae was back in the room and telling me I needed to get home before it got too late. As I stood, the minister stood also and said,

"Don't forget what I requested."

Tae looked puzzled and said, "What did you request, Dad?"

"That request was between Lou and me."

We walk out of the house and start toward my house. Tae asks me how I enjoyed my day with him, the church and his family. I say, "I really, really loved being with you all day long."

"Did you say love?"

"I did, Tae, say the word love."

"I like hearing you say that word. Can you say it again, but put the word "**I**" in front of it and the word "**you**" at the end of it?"

"No, I will not say those words in that order." We walk to my house and that warm feeling starts to stir in my lower body.

Chapter Ten

The pain from the beat down is so severe and I really need medical attention, but I do not want to make a request to the guards. I don't want to make any more people upset with me. I am trying to keep to myself and I do not want to offend a single soul. I am having conflicts with my old nature and my new nature. I am used to cussing, fighting and talking about people and enjoying seeing hurt feelings and tears coming from eyes. That was what I was about. What do you do when your old self has been stripped away? What I used to do to others, that horrible behavior is now directed toward me and I cannot believe I was so evil. I see the behavior and I look in the eyes of the offender and I see the reflection of myself in their eyes. I cannot believe how many times I was without compassion for my fellow man. I think back and I see the uncaring, heartless, inhuman evil animals and I just want to crawl in a hole and die. What is so horrific is that I behaved so grossly in front of my children. How can I be redeemed? I fall to the floor and stretch my hand out so far because I want to touch God in heaven. I know I have been a bad daughter, sister, aunt, and most of all a shameful mother.

~~~~~~

"Momma, I have changed." "Wait," she interrupts. "What kind of change?" "I turned my life over to Christ." "What the hell is wrong with you? The hell you say. You come in here, and fool, you dun turned on me. You know you wasn't raised like that, you damn fool."

~~~~~~

I cried that day when my son Lou told me he had found you. I can't believe I told him he was not raised to be a Christian. How can any mother say that to her child and be forgiven? I am a total mess. I am crying now because I have looked over my life and it so unbearable to relive. I am the worst example of a mother and how could I form the words to say, "You were not raised like that?" What? I was a negative example for my children and I did a horrible job of raising your precious gifts you gave to me. I am so sorry I do not have any words that I can say that will show the sadness I feel. **"Lord, can you forgive this trifling mother? Please have mercy on me."**

Granny Mo interrupts my prayer and says, "God will forgive you even if you have been a trifling mother. I don't mean to be listening. God told me to stop them from beating you.

I heard the request as clear as I am talking to you. I can tell you this; I was not the best mom. I did things that are just unspeakable."

I just remember this verse from 1 John 1:9, "If we confess our sins, He is faithful and just to forgive us our sins and to cleanse us from all unrighteousness."

"He is a prayer-answering God! What he has done for others he will do it for you. Just believe God, read, pray and obey his word to the best of your ability. Baby, we are human beings and not perfect. Everybody has done some things they regret. I don't know what you have done, but you are the most hated person in the jail. I got your back and I will try to look after you. I am just an old lady, most of the people respect me, and sometimes, what I say the people around here listen.

I was the type of woman wives hated. I was a home wrecker. I only fooled around with married men that made a six-figure income. I kept my mouth shut about what I did with the men and I was ok with playing my role as the other woman. I had affairs with men who had a lot to lose if word got out about their secret lives. I was paid well, I had a nice home, cars, trips, and I had it going on. If one of my clients moved to another city, died, or got tired of lying and cheating, a waiting list of men were at my disposal. I did not have a middleman, you know… a pimp, I worked the business alone. For years, I was doing well until one night my life turned and my good time came crashing down.

One rainy hot summer night, I was involved with a high-ranking official in the government. We were in his mansion in an exclusive suburban neighborhood that was gated in the Collierville Community. The elderly Jewish man's wife was out of the country, or so he thought. I heard a door open and the sound of high heels walking on the glossy marble floor. His wife was walking through the door. I heard the voice from the upstairs bedroom as she called, "Ruben, I am home." Two thumps hit the floor, I gathered it was a pair of luggage, and a set of keys hit a table. I heard the heels of her shoes coming up the stairs. I couldn't hide because… well, I was tied up to the post of the headboard with some fish net stockings. Ruben was gone to the drug store to get his blue pill prescription filled. I was not worried about being in this position long because he had done this before. Why he waited to go get the pills after

I was dressed in a tight teddy, I do not know. Anyway, she walked in the bedroom and did not say a word. I wanted to introduce myself and shake her hand, but I was not in a position to be courteous, so I just looked at her. She finally looked me in the eye, and shouted, "Tramp, where is my husband?"

"I can explain myself."

"Where is my husband?" she repeated.

"*Aaaa, he, he, he*, went to the drug store."

"Ooh, he is doing that!"

I heard the door slam, and he walked swiftly up the stairs. His wife backed up behind the open door. Ruben walked in shaking the big, clear, plastic prescription bottle in his right hand with a devilish smile on his face. "*Hot Chocolate*, I am going to make you scream my name." I know I had terror in my eyes, and my shoulders were pulled up to my ears, trying hard to warn him danger was lurking in the rear. He looked puzzled and said, "Wha, What's wrong?"

"Ruben, Ruben, Ruben, WHY?" His eyes bulged and his mouth opened showing his upper and lower dentures. He turned slowly to see his wife sobbing with her hands covering her mouth and eyes flooding with tears. I needed to make my escape, but my wrists were tied tight. I wiggled trying to free myself. I struggled, but I knew I would never be able to free myself. Ruben walked toward her and said, "Honey, she does not mean anything to me. I just met her and this is the first time, and we didn't even do anything. While I was at the store, I had made up my mind to tell her I could not do it."

"Do you take me for a fool? How were you going to make Hot Chocolate scream your name! Hunh!" Can you untie your whore and take my stocking off her and get her out of our bed?"

"Yes. Yes, let me do that!" He looked around the room in a panic as he tried to find something to use to untie me. I was thinking, *Fool, look in the second drawer of the nightstand and get the orange handled scissors.* His wife shouted, "Grab the scissors from the second drawer of the nightstand." As he snatched the scissors, his hands were shaking and I was afraid for the first time since this incident occurred. He looked in my eyes and he resembled a scared little boy. He cut the stocking and he reached towards me, but then he jerked his hand back. I brought my upper body forward and I pulled my legs together and stood upright. I reached for my jacket that was nearby; his wife said in a growling voice,

"Leave it whore!"

I walked toward the open door trying to pass her. As I passed her, she pushed me into the wall and I fell to the floor. I let that push go because I figured I deserved it being in the woman's home and even worse, tied up with her designer stocking stretched in her fancy bed. When I was trying to get up she bent over and spit in my face and called me a *black bitch!* I jumped up and punched her in her face and grabbed her by her silk shirt and threw her over the rails of the stairs. She fell through the glass coffee table below. I looked down and had no sympathy for her. Next thing I remembered was police running into the house, pistols drawn and Ruben stating, "This woman and a man were here when I came from the store. My wife must have startled them and one of them threw my wife over the banister. The black man that was on the stairs rushed past me and ran out the door." Ruben collapsed to the floor next to his wife's still body, crying uncontrollably.

"Well, I never disclosed what I was doing in the house in a teddy and what kind of business I was in. The detectives did not believe Ruben was telling the whole story; they said everything did not add up. The detective wondered how my income was so substantial and my lifestyle did not match my Consultant Firm position. I would not supply any clients' names and I did not ever say what really happened that night. I was sentenced to life in prison. I could not tell them I was a high priced call girl. I made some bad choices and I figured I did not need to involve any more people in my mess. Why am I telling you this sad story? I want you to know that if God forgave me He will do the same for you. Get your life together and get out of here and never come back. I will never leave jail. When I leave I will be rolled out in a body bag. I have never told a single person what really happened that hot rainy summer night." As tears roll down my face, I could tell she was silently crying. "You are still young. Please, live a productive life; don't waste your life in this place."

I was so sad for Granny Mo, as I lay on the cot and I could see my life falling into the very same trap. I close my eyes and try to stop seeing the image of Granny Mo tossing the wife onto the glass table.

Chapter Eleven

I am feeling like I want to take our relationship to a more intimate level. I am tired of playing the nice girl role. It was fun, but I want to do more than kiss his lips. Tae seems very satisfied to just kiss and rub his fingers through my hair. Occasionally he will grab my waist tight, but then he will take his hands away real fast. It seems after meeting his mother and his overprotective father telling me I been around, he really got on my nerves. I did not like that comment. It was as if he knew I was trying hard to be a good girl, but he could tell that role was not going to last. He was right. I am starting to think about my sexual urges and when I am around Tae the floodgate bursts open.

Tae states he wants to wait until he is married. He has asked me what school do I think he needs to go to because he wants me to follow him to the same college. I do not know about all this college business, but I am getting restless with all this kissing. I need to figure out how to get Tae to do it with me one time and I will not have to worry after that because he will have the constant urge and will not be able to resist me.

Sammie Lee comes in the house with a small bottle that's wrapped in a brown bag, lodged in his back pocket. He strolls in and puts two fingers in the air, chin and head raised at the same time. I watch him as he goes to the kitchen, opens the cabinet door and pulls a large slender coffee cup from the cabinet and places it on the flowered tablecloth that has a few small tears along the corners. He pulls the brown bag from his pocket and pours some of the contents in the cup. He carefully tucks the bag down in his pocket. He sits down at the table only speaking after he takes two small swallows.

"Louvenia let me hold a five. Don't say you don't have any money. You hang out with the smarty-pants preacher boy. Yesterday was Sunday, I know you gave him some and I bet you got some of the money for the offering tray yesterday. We need to both get paid from him; what's our plan? Cause, I know you have no interest in the church boy."

"What are you talking about? I like him."

"Yea right," he says as he sips from the cup. "We need to get together on our plan." He gulps the last of his drink. "I better get out of here before your grandmomma and my mother get up and come in here and find me drinking in the kitchen." He puts down the cup and walks right out of the front door. I look at the cup and right away I figure how

I can get real close to Tae.

Two days later, I put alcohol in a metal gray thermos bottle with cherry Kool-Aid added to it. I lured Tae down to the basement and gave him two honey buns. Without fail he is always hungry and thirsty after practice. He was reluctant at first, but he followed me because he liked to see me in the blue jeans and my tight red top. He ate the two honey buns and downed the liquids in the thermos so fast he was instantly happy and a bright smile crossed over his handsome face. He was standing and laughing uncontrollably. He was dancing near me and grabbed me and twirled around me twice. He looked at me and said, "You so pretty, girl and you my girl." He starts sweating as he pulled me very close, kissing me very passionate like he never did before. I grabbed his pants and with one pull his pants were down. He said with a shout, "No, No!" I whispered very softly, "Do you want me?" He said, "Yes, yes, yes!" I watch his eyes as I slowly pull down my super tight jeans. I can see his impatient upper body wiggle. I touch him and before I knew it we were close, real close. After a short time, Tae was crying and saying, "No, no, this was not supposed to happen until we got married. I should not have done this to you, I am sorry! God I am sorry; this is not what I should have done. We need to get away from down here." We both pull up our clothes and walk up the stairs. I grab the honey bun wrappers from the bench and throw them both in my already heavy backpack.

We walk together in silence. As we continue to walk up the stairs, I see Mister Nosey Thompson. He looks at me and as he passes, he says, "The mole is back; haven't seen you in a while." I look at Tae and his face is so sad and his eyes are wet from quiet tears. I don't think he heard what the janitor was saying. I know he did not hear him when he said, "Looks like she's going to mess that good boy up." When we walk out of school, Tae says in a low voice, "I must go by the church and kneel at the altar. Can you ever forgive me? I look at him with downcast eyes and could only shake my head. As he walked off, I knew I would never have that loving guy again. I remember the words of his father, about not putting traps in his son's path. I felt so sad and my heart was breaking into very little pieces as I walked home alone.

47

Chapter Twelve

Two days later after being absent from school I didn't have the courage to look at Tae as he stood beside my locker. He looked at me and said, "Sweetie, have you been sick? I tried to call you several times. What, did you have a cold?" Mabel walked up, Tae faced her and said, "Hey Mabel, did you tell your sister I tried to call her several days to check on her?"

She softly said, "Yes, I told her you called, and I told her you wanted her to call you." A loud strained voice came over the intercom, "All students report immediately to your homeroom." Tae looked at me and said, "Meet me here after last period." I nodded, and walked to my homeroom. I was feeling funny and I worried that my period, which is never late, had not arrived.

The hallway was empty and Tae seemed to be angry because he had been waiting a long time for me. "Why are you trying to avoid me?" "I am not. We had a short cheer meeting, and I have to get back to turn in my uniform. Can you meet me at Douglass Park in about an hour?"

"Ok, sweetie, whatever you say." I had already turned in my uniform to the squad captain; my task now is to go to Rexall's and pick up a pregnancy kit. I buy the kit and go straight to the restroom. I open the kit and throw the unused packaging in the garbage. As I toss my hand toward the garbage, I see a stick in the can that showed whoever was in here before me had a test result of negative. I take my finger and touch my forehead each shoulder and my heart before dropping pee on the stick. I close my eyes and I open my eyes to a positive sign. I take a short breath and walk out of the restroom and down the store aisle and straight out the door.

I arrive before Tae. I am sitting on the table that is full of graffiti and Tae walks up with a smile on his face. I look at him and say softly, "I am quitting you."

"What? Stop, playing girl. I am sorry for what happen in the restroom"

"Shh! I put liquor in your Kool-Aid; you were high and I took advantage of you. I don't want to have anything to do with you. I was trying to loosen you up. There is no way I would want you any longer. What we did, did not feel good. You act like a girl and afterward you told me you had to go to the altar. I need a real boyfriend and not one who is scared to *get it!* I wasted all this time being your sweetie and this

48

is what I got from you."

I just wanted to tell him I really do like you. I was holding back the tears behind that lie. "You were popular and I wanted to be known just a little bit better. I was so tired of just kissing and what happened the other day was a waste of my good stuff! What you need is a good old church girl. I tried to hang, but damn, I can't stand to be with you another second."

"You can't tell me what we had was fake. I don't know what is going on but something has changed you. Don't do this to us. I forgive you for spiking my drink. I know I was upset about that, I have gotten past that, and I want us to move past this. *What can I do to make this better? "Please, give me a chance."*

"You can do one thing for me, Tae."

"Anything, sweetie!"

"You can get out of my face, and forget you ever met me. When I look at you, you make my flesh crawl.

Tae's face looked so sad and defeated, he searched my face and I could tell he was fighting back tears. I turned just in time before the tears dropped. I swiftly walked down the path past the tall green metal slide. I wanted to run off a cliff. I knew my life would never be the same and I would never love anyone like I love my Tae. Well, I will love baby Tae, with all my heart because I did not want to stop this guy from going off to college and being somebody. He would do the right thing if he knew I was carrying his baby, but I don't want him in my life, because I chose to take sexual advantage of him. I have to live with that choice. His father was right when he said I had been around. I took a deep breath and said, "I don't need nobody!" I dried my face and said, "I will never tell Tae or his family about this baby. I don't need his little saintly family looking crazy at me. I got this!"

Chapter Thirteen

Momma didn't pay the rent and we are told we must leave within in 48 hours. It has been only a day since I quit Tae and this is good news to my ears. I will change schools and we will live in a smaller rental house across town. Mabel refused to move with us. She wants to stay with friends so she can graduate with her class. I can't believe Grandmomma is allowing her to make this arrangement. Our mother couldn't care less what she does or what any of her children do. Mabel has started to get on my nerves again. The resentment seems to have increased ever since I stopped seeing Tae. The bitterness for her has resurfaced and I don't know why I had started being nice to her. She wants to finish her last year at the high school since she only has two months before she graduates. Mabel is going out of town to go to college and I can't wait. The whole family knows she is leaving the city to go to college, even though she was offered a full scholarship, because she is shamed of us. I say to her, "Go! Don't nobody care about your flat behind. Good riddance to you!"

We are packing things in boxes and brown bags and trying to finish clearing out everything in the house before the deadline. If we do not finish, the sheriff will come and throw our stuff on the curb, tossing our things without any regard. This has happened to us so many times; when you miss the deadline, the people seem to be angry you did not have the place empty like you were told. It's like they are on a deadline and they refuse to hear any excuses. We have gone through evictions before so I am determined to have everything out, floor swept, mopped, counters in the kitchen and bathroom are wiped off and the crappy place has been inspected. Mabel, of course, is trying to organize the household contents by rooms. She has markers and is giving out orders to the younger ones from a chart she has color coded on a white notepad. I finally took all I could from her. I cussed her out and pushed her out the front screen door and told her to go on to her new fake family.

Grandmomma is tired and she is sitting down again. It looks like every ten minutes she has to rest her swollen feet. We are almost finished packing and Momma and Sammie Lee come in the house drunk. They both are laughing in a hushed manner, crouching down and walking unsteady. They come in announcing they are here to help and insist on moving boxes and bags to the car right outside on North Hollywood.

We all wish the two of them would go away and not interfere in the last details of our packing. Grandmomma just stares and does not make one comment. The silent treatment is like getting a tongue-lashing; you never want Grandmomma to stare and not make one single comment. It was a sign of her displeasure of the behavior she was witnessing. A young deacon from the church is here to help move our things to our new place.

The three younger brothers and two younger sisters act as though we are on an adventure. This moving around from place to place is getting old, but I can have this baby and no one will know, only a few people will know that Tae is the father. I guess when I can't hide the baby any longer I will tell Momma and Grandmomma. Tae and his family will never know about this baby. His father will never say I laid a trap for his son.

Mabel came over on Saturday to visit us at our new apartment, and all the hate I had for her had returned, especially when she brought up Tae's name. She wanted to know why I quit him, and said that he was visibly sad all the time. She said she tried to avoid him because he was constantly asking about you and your whereabouts. "He told me he walked over to our old house and wondered when we moved. He was so confused and did not know why I was not with the family." She said she had no answer for him, especially when he said his heart was breaking. She wanted to know what she should tell him. I cussed her alfro-wearing, wanna-be-somebody self, plumb out. I told her I was nice to her because I was with Tae but I was back and she needed to get her fake flat ass out of my face. I could feel the evil rising up in me and I was happy. She got so mad she ran out the door crying.

Two months later the valedictorian and the salutatorian were listed in the paper and the colleges they were going to attend. Mabel was first and Tae was second in their class ranking out of 400 seniors. The family was happy for Mabel and we all were supposed to go to the graduation. I was getting slightly bigger in the middle so I did not want Tae or his family examining me as I came to an event I did not have any desire to attend. While the family was gone to the graduation I was trying to see where I could go and get a quick high. The guys in this new neighbor-hood would give dope to ladies if you would do favors for them. I was ready. Bruce was the first guy I walked up to and he said, "What's up Papersack?" Some people in the hood call me this because my complexion resembles a paper sack bag; at this point, I don't care I just want to get high.

I said, "You got it, Big Daddy! Can you help a sister out? I need to touch the clouds. I have one problem: no money."

"You know what I want from you. Can I get that? Papersack, did you hear me? Let's go in the alley; it's crawling time." A tear dropped from my left eye and the old me that loved being in ecstasy was back.

Tae and I are gazing in each other's eyes and I am thinking while smiling at him that he really cares for me. He wants to be with me and he enjoys holding my hand and just talking and listening.

I thought about the unborn baby growing inside of me and I felt a loneliness that covered my body like a cloud. I knew I would never again have a guy like my Tae. If this baby is a boy, I will always think about Tae, but he and his family will never know about this child.

Chapter Fourteen

My feet are swelling, head and my ribs hurt every time I breathe. Granny Mo has told her life story and I am not in the mood for sad stories. I do not know what to do with myself. I can't bear to lie down or stand up. It's telephone time and I need to call somebody in my family. I know I said I did not want my family to know where I am, but I am hurting and I need to call somebody because I believe I have some broken parts and I need medical attention right away. Granny Mo called out, "Louvenia, you need to make use of your phone privilege and don't let them tell you that you can't use the phone."

I am the next person to use the phone and I am trying to think of whom I need to call. I could call Mabel or I could call my son, Louvious. Lou has to be upset that I ran out of the church and embarrassed him in front of the whole church. I have never been a good sister to Mabel and I call her every time I am in trouble. I have never thought about how she feels about helping me. Other people's emotions have never been something I regarded. I am hurting and I am ashamed to have to involve somebody in my stuff. I guess I will call Mabel; it is Saturday and I hope she is at home. The phone rings twice and she answers, "Hello, Pruitt's residence.

"Mabel! Hello, this is Louvenia." My voice cracks with sad emotion.

"Louvenia! Where are you?"

"I am in the Penal Farm. What? Yes, I have been here for six months. The bail was too high and I just did not want to ask you for any more money to get me released."

"What have you been charged with? Do you have an attorney, and when is your scheduled trial date?"

"Mabel, I have been beaten bad by a gang of prisoners and I need medical attention right now."

"I am getting ready to come right now and I will call Winton to meet me out there. We will take care of this; don't worry, your family is on the way. Lou, I love you and we will be out there in less than an hour."

It's been a long time since I felt anyone cared about me and I was able to feel the love and not take what someone was going to do for me for granted. I have not been kind to Mabel for most of my life. How can she continue to look past my evil heart and help me without a lecture or judgment? I feel like the sun is shining on me and peace has replaced pain. This is better than any high or any sexual experience I have ever had. I know, Lord, I got to do better. Stealing, drugging, sexual encounters, fighting and just being a horrible person are things I must stop doing to be a new me. I have a lot to do to change and I know I will not be able to do anything without the help of God. "Lord, please help me!" I pray silently, dropping on my knees. I am feeling relaxed and I can lie down on the bed and feel comfortable like someone is rocking me in the pit of their arms. I close my eyes and I fall asleep.

The guard awakens me from an amazing sleep. The slumber was so good I thought it was the next morning, but it has been less than two hours. The guard tells me I have two visitors: one is Attorney Winton Pruitt and the other a female who is saying she is your sister. I get up feeling pain as I swing my legs off the bed and onto the floor. I limp down the hall to the visitor meeting area and I see my sister and brother-in-law. Mabel looks at me and gasps as she sees the multiple bruises on my body.

"What happened to you?" Mabel asked.

"I was beat up by a group of inmates, and the guards did not do a thing." Her husband barely looks at me, when he sternly demands to see the warden. He was told the warden was not at work and he shouts, "Get him on the phone immediately, because my client needs urgent medical attention." I look at Mabel and then at the guard. I am stunned that the guards are running around as this short chubby man shouts out instructions.

The next thing I know I am on a gurney and I am being put in an ambulance. I hear Winton tell the attendant, "Take her to John Gaston Hospital." Mabel and one of the female guards get in the ambulance with me and her husband follows in his car right behind the speeding medical vehicle. I tell Mabel as I try to speak without emotionally breaking down, "Mabel, how can you love a person like me? I don't how you can care for a person like me who is so unlovable. If I had been you I would have given up on me a long time ago, I just want to thank you for being the best sister any person like me could have. You have been nothing but what a Christian is supposed to be. Your husband made all this possible. I know God has guided both of you to be the kind of people He wants all His followers to be. I have not been a good sister or mother." Mabel puts her index finger on her thick lips and says, "Lay back and rest."

We arrive at the hospital and the driver jumps out and swings the back doors open. In one swoop, I am dropped to the paved parking lot on the narrow cot. I am rolled down through a tunnel leading to the hospital and up the elevator to a small curtained room. I am so shocked to see a man is there sitting in a chair.

~~~~~~

I was standing over the bed when my grandmomma was dying. She told me that she was tired and she was going home. I said, "You are too weak to go to the house."

"I will never leave this hospital alive," my grandmomma said, "Everybody claims when you get a certain age and you come to Gaston, you don't make it out of here"

~~~~~~

I am rolled into this semi-darkened room and I see a figure of a man standing in the shadows.

I can't believe whom I see. Tears run down my face and I close my eyes in disbelief.

Chapter Fifteen

My grandmomma looks at me as I walk in the house from school, my books held with two hands covering my stomach. She motions for me to come to the chair where she's sitting. As I walk toward her I grip the books sitting on my stomach closer. She looks at my neck and says, "Ho mun months is you?" I can't believe she's asking me this. I look with my best, "What?" look. "When las time you buy Kotex?" I can't lie and confess in a low tone with my eyes downward, "Four months." "Yo go to healfy depar tomorrow."

She gets up from the chair unsteady, grabs hold of the silver walker and walks at a faster than usual rate down the hall. As I watch this aged soul, she does not utter a sound. Her body becomes a blur as I continue to stare long after she disappears around corner of the narrow hallway. She is the first person I admit to that I am having a baby.

We are in the clinic and my name is called. As I walk toward the clerk I see Rev. Robinson sitting reading the newspaper. As I walk I try to suck my belly in that is protruding out. He looks directly at my stomach. I look straight at him and give him the head nod. He looks over his thick coke cola wired glasses. I know he knows I am pregnant and I hope he does not tell his son. The young white doctor confirmed what I already know. I am mad that the good Rev. saw me and I am mad he was right about me. Doctor Webby asks me what age did I start having sex and how many sexual partners have I had. I told him, "None of your damn business. Sir, can you leave out so I can get dressed, and I can get the hell out of here?" As I put my clothes on I look in the metal drawer and take out two boxes of bandages and tissues, five tongue depressors, two thermometers and three rolls of toilet paper. I scramble around in the second drawer and there are more things to steal and my eyes light up. I hear footsteps and the rap on the door only gives me time to shut the second drawer and conceal my newfound treasures in my backpack.

A nurse comes in and asks if I would like to talk. She says she's been in my shoes and she can give me some tips on how to maneuver through this tough journey. She asks me if I know who the father is and if I think he would be supportive in bringing up this child. I tried to give this red cow a pass, as I smile at her with fake compassion. My grandmomma was sitting in the waiting room, so I tried to resist taking my anger about this baby out on this middle-aged heifer.

"Look I know exactly who fathered this baby! What, you think I am a whore and do not know which of the many males I slept with could be my baby's daddy? I was with one guy and one guy only. Does that help you with the note you need to write up on me to put in my file? You think I am stupid? I know the doctor told you to come and talk to me 'cause you had a baby out of wedlock, so he makes you talk to the poor black teenager." I move closer to her and say, "Get your flunky ass out of my face! Now go tell the doc what I said and write that exact quote in my medical file." I push past her, brushing against her shoulder hard as I walk down the hall. I looked for Rev. Robinson and a little child was sitting in the chair he once occupied. I walked over to my grandmother and I helped her raise up from the too small chair. She struggles to pull up, bending forward at her waist and she manages to stand slightly upright.

We walk slowly to the bus stop. After waiting a few minutes we ascend the stairs and slide into the first row of seats on the 10 Hollywood going to the Douglass Community. We get off the bus and Momma is in front of the Piggy Wiggly. She is standing outside the door begging from exiting customers. She is holding a tin green bean can with the giant green man on the label. She tries to hide the can as we approach, but decides not to, holding the can and continuing to beg from everyone entering and leaving. Grandmomma says one word, "Why?" as she takes awkward steps, dragging her walker as her pocketbook sways from the left side.

I look at this lady that carried me in her womb and I realize for the first time that I am carrying a child. I wonder will I be the type of mother this person is that I barely know. Will I be a duplicate of her? My heart grieves and I know the answer; I will be just like the woman I see before me.

I remember being in a fight in the seventh grade with a girl who lived on Jackson Avenue. She called me a dumb hoe and I told her to meet me in the grassy field after school. Big Sue put a small stick on my shoulder and one on Keesha's shoulder. She ran over to me and knocked the stick off my shoulder. I hit her one time in the face and she fell to the ground and was out like a light. She fell and some brown stuff appeared on the back of her pants as she laid face down in the grass. I was looking and I smelled this foul odor. Big Sue screamed out, "Girl, you knocked the shit out of her. Wow, that's where that saying came from!" I feel a little bad as I go over and get her up and say to her, "Don't ever call me hoe again. Yo mama is a hoe." and I walked off.

Momma is calling my name. "Girl, I ain't gon' tell you again. Go on home with your grandmomma; you 'bout to stop my hustle I got goin' on." I walked away and I knew I would be just like my mother.

Chapter Sixteen

I am on the stretcher in John Gaston Hospital and in the shadows I see my son Lou. Tears roll down my face as I look at the son that I used to help me get all the things I wanted in all kinds of criminal ways. He is a preacher and he looks so handsome. I can't believe he is here to see a woman that was cruel to him when he told me he had been called to preach. How could I abandon him? I never went back to visit him in jail. I was drunk that day like I was every time I came to visit him in prison. I would drink several forty ounces and ride the bus to the jailhouse. I was an embarrassment to him; I knew it, but I did not care. How could he be standing here with his hands stretched out to me a second time? He was in the church with his hands out, trying to bring me out from the world. I failed him that day when I walked the aisle and ran away from God and him. He had a tear stained face then and he has one now. I am ready to change and be the woman God and my son will not be ashamed.

If Lou forgave the people who put him in jail, including his girl-friend Sheree who now is his wife, I can forgive my grandfather. I can't let my grandfather continue to destroy my mind and self-respect. I pray, "Lord, you know me and all that I have ever done. Please forgive me and give me the strength and the courage to begin to be a better person. Lord, take away my obsessions of stealing, drinking, drugs, fighting, cursing, sexual urges and anything not pleasing to you. Before I could say Amen, Lou sang out in a long cadence, "Amen!" I did not realize I was praying out loud. I stretched out my hand and Lou grabbed my shoulders and pulled me toward his big broad shoulders and said, "Momma, are you ready to give your life to Christ?"

I cried in his arms and said, "Reverend, I am ready."

He asked, "Do you repent of your sins and believe Jesus died on the cross to save you?

I said, "Yes, I repent of my sins and I believe Jesus died on the cross to save me."

He cried out with joy, "Momma, you are saved!"

I felt no pain from my injuries and I felt like a baby, restored and revived; it felt like all my problems and addictions were slowly fading away. For the first time in a long time I felt a sense of hope. For years I did not have it and I lost some when I lost my first son, Tae and when I walked away from his father Big Tae. No other child or man could replace the love I had for those two men. Now I know… do not put anyone or thing before the love of God.

Lou said, "Momma, Sheree and I have been looking everywhere for you. I thank God Mabel called me and told me you were arrested the day you ran out of church and you have been there ever since. We are going to get you the medical treatment you need." I saw a person move and I did not realize that one of the prison guards was in the room. How did she get here? I guess she must have been in the ambulance that brought me to the hospital. She was always mean and looked the other way when any fight broke out. She moves closer when Lou asks me how I got the bruises and the injuries. The doctor came in and asked if everyone could step out while he examined me. Lucy, the young weave wearing, woman with the tight uniform and fake eyelashes that could cool off a small room spoke up and said, "I cannot leave the prisoner."

The doctor said, "I cannot examine her while you are in the room. You can sit outside the room; I will take responsibility for her while she is in this room. When I am finished I will turn her back over to your capable hands." Before she could say anything, he walked to the open door and said, "Thank you!" She walked slowly out looking back at me with a frown on her face. As she passed through the door he slammed the door shut.

The short doctor with the dark complexion, and the thick accent introduced himself as Doctor Abdu Mohan. He asked if I was wounded in jail and if it was by the inmates or the guards. He asked when it oc-curred. He was outraged when he found out it had happened several days ago as he jotted down all the details. He examined me and he told me just looking, it appeared I had a broken wrist, severe injuries to my stomach and some lacerations to my head and to the left side of my body.

The nurse came in and Doctor Mohan told her to page the on-call social worker, *stat*. The doctor told the nurse I needed to be scheduled for an X-ray and an MRI. The two left the exam room and Mabel, Win-ton, Lou, and the guard came back in the room. I told Mabel I was so sorry for all the times I was such a lousy sister. I told her I couldn't be-lieve how she could continue to be such a wonderful person when I was such a horrible sister. I looked over to Winton and told him he has been nothing but loving to me and I didn't show him the love he deserved. I was wiping the tears from my eyes and the hospital transporter came in, asked my name and checked my armband. The bed was rolled out of the room and down the hall, and of course the dumb guard was walking beside the male transporter.

Two hours later, I was rolled back and Rev. Worthy was in the room and he stood as my bed entered the room. He walked over and asked how I was doing.

I said, "I am fine," gazing down at the floor. He grabbed my hand and asked if the group would gather, touching, for a word of prayer. Pastor Worthy prayed for me and when he finished, everyone in the room was wiping their eyes. I thanked him and he shook everyone's hand and walked out of the room.

The doctor was coming in as Pastor Worthy was leaving out. He was looking at a chart and stated that there seemed to be some damage to the kidney. He said he wanted to run some more tests, but he needed some of my siblings to see if they were a match for a kidney transplant should the need arise. Lou howled out and said, "If my mother will need a new kidney; I will give her mine."

The doctor spoke up and said, "This is only a precautionary procedure. We must test the biological sibling first to get the best possible match." Mabel stood up and said, "Test me also, I want to see if I am a match; if one is needed, I am willing."

Doctor Mohan told Mabel to go down to the first floor so that the lab could start the first round of screenings. Mabel picked up her purse, moved closer to the bed, kissed me on my forehead and stated she would be back soon. She looked over at Winton; in a second he jumped up and followed his wife out of the cramped hospital room.

Chapter Seventeen

I have been a sorry Momma. I can't stand to think of how I raised my children. I started by denying my oldest child Martavious the knowledge of who was his father. I love his father and the child we produced. My heart did not have enough room for anyone, not even the man I married, Jack Johnson. Jack was a loving man when we first got together. He did not mind that I already had a small child, and he loved him like he was his own child. We both got jobs and we had good money coming in the house. I started taking the extra money and using it on drinking and getting high. At first, we only got high on Saturday nights, then it was on Fridays and Saturdays and then it progressed to the whole weekend. After a short time it was every night and eventually every morning, noon and night. The babies started coming and eventually we lost our jobs. Fighting, cursing, stealing, evictions, moving and soon our hope and dignity were gone.

Jack started staying out late and then he would not come home for days. I would put his butt out and I would let him come and go and I was unable to say, "No, not again." I didn't ever really love him but I could not bear to be without a man. I always thought I had to have some sort of guy who seemed to love me and I wanted some small control over him, no matter how small. If I thought I was losing my perceived control, I would get mad and cuss and start fights—physically or verbally.

I can't believe how I behaved when Lou first told me he had been called to preach. I was so angry that he chose to be a minister; I could only think of how my grandfather took my innocence away from me. All the women in the family knew he was a dirty old man. They only tried to block me from this devil but never said a single word of confrontation to him. How can people of God let a so-called man of God do this to a child? One hot Sunday evening after church I heard one of my older female relatives in the kitchen just before the weekly family meal say, "That's what men folk do." I have never forgotten that phrase. Are the women supposed to excuse this kind of behavior from men? I carried that saying around with me and I made irresponsible decisions about how I allowed the men in my life to disrespect me because I believed that's how they behaved.

It's a new day! I will no longer allow a man to treat me as if I do not matter. I will be respected or he has to quickly move on. I think to myself, can I do it? I can and I will. I am one of God's gifts and He would not be pleased if I didn't expect anything but the best treatment for his jewel.

~~~~~~

I am going to get my life together; drinking and drugging have been a way of life for me that must stop. I will try and get in the drug program at Lou's church and I pray to cease abusing my body. I am coming out of my trance and I am ushered back to the room. I see my five grown children.

They all rush toward me and give me a big bear hug. The nurse walks in and says visiting hours are over and the family must leave. As I look around the room I ask, "Where is Sammie Lee? Is he somewhere in the restroom with a bottle in his hand?" The room is silent and all heads drop downward as if on cue. As if they had rehearsed for this very moment. Lou moves from Sheree his wife and moves closer to me, grabbing my hand and slightly clearing his throat. I watch my family and all have tears dropping on the white tiled floor.

"Momma, Sammie Lee died three months ago."

"You are lying; my brother is not dead. I would know! He not dead, he not dead. Why are you telling me that? He's in the bathroom. Sammie Lee, bring yourself out and stop playing jokes. This is a mean joke you tryin' to pull on me. I am getting out of this bed and look in the restroom. If he not there I know what alley he hangs out at. Give me my damn clothes so I can go look for my brother. Y'all don't know what y'all talkin' about."

The intercom blurts out, "Visiting hours are over. All visitors must depart the building at this time." The nurse quietly speaks out, "I know some family issues need to be discussed, but you have to continue this matter tomorrow. Momma is screaming, "My Sammie is not gone! The brother I love!"

As the family walks out of the room and pass the nurses station, they hear on an intercom device that a shot is needed stat to calm the patient in room 642.

Chapter Eighteen

The next morning the nurse comes in to tell me Dr. Abdu Mohan will be in my room a little later after he finishes up his rounds for the morning. She says he will give me the results of the battery of tests that were run. I look at her in a puzzled way, and ask her, "Who are you and where am I?"

"I am Mary your nurse and you are in the hospital. You are being treated for some injuries you sustained." I try to remember several details of my life, but nothing is there. The nurse asks, "What day is it?" I do not know. She asks, "What is your name and birthdate?" I cannot remember; I am unable to answer. Suddenly a tall young man walks in the room with a nice black suit on and a wide smile. I have no idea of the identity of this nicely dressed man.

"Good morning, Momma. How are you?" I look at him and say, "Who are you calling Momma?" The doctor comes in the room and the nurse motions for Dr. Mohan to step into the hallway. I look over this tall man who was coming over to the bed and was trying to see who the woman was talking to in the wrinkled, dingy lab coat. As the tall man grabs my shoulder, I scream in terror and the whispering couple comes rushing back in the room. "He is touching me and I don't know who this dreadlock-wearing rascal is. Help me! Keep him away from me, trying to touch all over me."

The nurse touches the man on his shoulder and leads him out of the room. The doctor asks, "Do you feel any pain anywhere?" I say, "No!" "Do you remember being in a fight in the prison?"
I tell him I can't remember hardly anything, but I am not the kind of person that's been to jail.
"What is going on with me?" He looks at his clipboard and says, "You have several breaks in both legs, your left hip has been knocked out of place and you have several contusions over your body. Those problems I just mentioned are mendable; I am concerned about the memory loss." "What's causing it?" "I am not sure; it may be the medication or the traumatic family news you received yesterday." "What news?" "Let's take care of the injuries and the memory loss first, and then we will have a family member come and talk to you."

"Doc, am I going crazy or is this an early sign of dementia? Tell me, tell me," I demand as my voice elevates and tears are dropping all over the pillow. I am so afraid; I can't remember who I am. "I don't even know what I look like. Bring me a mirror so I can see what I look like. I demand a mirror right damn now."

The doctor walks closer to me as the nurse gives him the mirror. I look and I scream to the top of my lungs and say, "I am old and my hair is gray. My God, I don't know this woman with the mole on her nose. Everybody get out right now! Get out and let me be by myself." Lou walks over and cries, "Momma!" "Hurry up and get that nappy-headed fool outta here."

Doctor Mohan points to the door and walks forward and all follow him. Lou has his hands over his mouth and says, "What happened to my mother in this short sixteen hours? She was a little distraught, but she had her memory. Can someone tell me *something?*" "I am not sure of what's going on. It may be head trauma from the fight, reaction from medication, or a psychological ordeal from the distressing news of the death of her brother. A second full MRI scan will be conducted and the test will give us a better idea of why there is memory loss. Do you have any further questions?" "No, not at this time. I am going home and call a family meeting."

Three hours later the adult family members gathered to discuss the status of Louvenia's criminal case as well as her memory loss and physical injuries from the altercation at the prison. Lou started the meeting off with prayer with everyone holding hands in a circle with heavy hearts and bowed heads.

Winton discussed the legal problems facing Louvenia. He informed the family that she has a pending court date in the next two weeks but in light of the new medical issues, he will ask for a continuance until the medical issues are resolved. Mabel questioned the memory loss and Lou explained about the tests that had been ordered and said the results would be discussed as soon as they are available. Vanessa, one of Lou's oldest sisters wanted to know if their mother had been told any more information about Sammie Lee. Lou did not say a word; he just moved his head from side to side several times with closed eyes. Mabel wanted the family to know that she and Winton had discussed Lou coming to stay at her house after she is discharged from the hospital. Her husband had secured bail for her to get out of prison until her trial. The family meeting ended with Mable praying and asking God to take care of her sister's legal and medical problems and to comfort the entire family.

Chapter Nineteen

Two months have passed and Louvenia's memory has not returned and she is agitated most of the time. She has lost hope and is severely depressed and does not want to interact socially with anyone. The memory loss and both her legs being in a cast have not made her a joyful person to be around. She prefers to stay in one of Mabel's bedrooms that was restored to be a very pleasant, warm and bright colorful place for her sister. Louvenia stays in the room most days in the bed with the blinds drawn and the lights off.

The day has come for Louvenia to begin the process of her trial. She has been charged with the theft of less than 500 dollars. Testimony of time spent in jail, counseling sessions with the psychiatrist, fight incident, medical attention denied, physical injuries and the loss of memory accounting for the time served was the end to all legal battles. Louvenia, hearing all the various witnesses that spoke during the trial, was so overwhelmed that she wept quietly, uncontrollably throughout the trial. The trial lasted only two days and she was released and free to go with time served. Judge Webster apologized for the justice system failing to protect her and the legal rights that were denied. The eyes of Louvenia seem to light up and she was asked to make a statement. The family was afraid of what she would say when the microphone was handed to her.

Louvenia said, "I thank you for your words of apology. You did not have to do it. I was a thief, abuser of alcohol and drugs and not a good role model for my children. I listened to the testimony of all the things that happened to me in jail and my memory started slowly coming back. I was weeping during the various people who talked about me and I was so saddened. All these things that happened to me, I have no regrets and I will not look back. God spoke to me during the trial and He said, 'I was with you during the time you did not want to receive me, but I have prepared you for this appointed time.' I am testifying to all here that God is in my life and I give God all the glory and praise. I thank God, my family, and you, Judge Webster. I am a changed person and I am thankful for your verdict and most of all the help and the care of my family who came to my defense even willing to give me a kidney that I didn't have to have. I am truly blessed and I will be the best law-abiding citizen I can be."

The judge said, "If there are no further comments, this case is dismissed."

Lou and Sheree walked up to Louvenia and together they strolled out of the courtroom. The family was outside in the hallway crying and praising God for what they witnessed in the courtroom.

What a wonderful celebration carried on as they continued their way down the stairs and out of the doors to the parking lot. Songs were sung and prayers were offered up to the heavenly Father. After thirty minutes the group agreed to go to the church and stand before the altar and praise God, the provider and protector.

Chapter Twenty

Six months later on a Saturday evening in the basement of New Christian Holiness Tabernacle Church we celebrated Louvenia 55th birthday. Her legs have healed and most of her memory has been restored. She is dressed in an elegant dress that is nicely fitted and she has discarded the many wigs and like her sister she is sporting a nicely cut curly hairstyle. The gray curls give her a look that is so beautiful that it has transformed her appearance and life. The party was so joyful with lively music, songs, food and the many guests made Louvenia so happy and grateful. She was showered with so many wonderful gifts and money. Lou announced to his mother that a surprise guest was about to enter the room. He told her the person had been trying to find her for over thirty years. Mabel had a smile on her face, trying to figure out who has been looking for her for that long. She sat up in her chair and waited as the doors opened and a tall man walked through the door.

I can't believe my eyes as this tall handsome man walks toward me with a receding hairline and slightly mingling gray and black strands. The bowlegged, handsome guy with a pearly white, slight-gap smile walked slowly toward me. The tears quickly filled my eyes and I was so shocked and in disbelief, I could not speak. He said, "Hello, sweetie!" He bent down and kissed me on my cheek and said, "Happy Birthday!" I stared for a long time and his big hand grabbed mine and he kissed my hands like he did when he first met me so many years ago. The whole room broke out in applause and I was brought back from the past to the present. The music started and my attention was focused back on my first love. Winton, my brother-in-law interrupted my stare and said, "I hope you don't mind. I saw Attorney Martavious Robinson at a legal conference last week and we were talking and I told him about your birthday party. I hope you don't mind me taking the liberty of inviting an old acquaintance. He flew in from Boston last night and stayed at our house."

"What a wonderful surprise! Brother-in-law, I do not mind; I am delighted." A slow jam comes on and Tae asks if I want to two-step. I say, "Yes, why not!"

"Louvenia, you better be glad we are in the church, because I would ask you to slow dance with me so I could have your pretty self close to me."

"What would your wife have to say about that request?"

"If I had a wife she would not like it, but since I do not have one, I can make any comment I want to a former girlfriend. Now what will your husband have to say about me flirting with you?"

"Oh, is that what you are doing?"

"Yes, I am trying to get my rap on. Now, what about your husband or your man?"

"Do you see some brother all up on me?"

"No, I just want to know because I keep looking all around."

"Relax, Tae you have no worries in that area."

"Good, we have some uninterrupted catching up to do."

Suddenly, people stop dancing and a circle gathers around Tae and me. Happy Birthday was shouted out and Sheree my beautiful daughter in law led the song. I was so happy, happier than I have ever been in my life. I did not want this peaceful, joyful time to end. I was escorted to a table full of envelopes of all sizes and colors and bright shiny presents. I began tearing open the boxes and Mabel was taking notes so I could send the thank you notes that she already had in a pink basket along with a book of stamps. Mabel has always had a good heart; she loved to organize parties and she did a good job putting this event together. I wonder why I hated her and told her constantly she was not any kin to us. She has done a lot for me as well as all my children. Even though I was a terrible person and I was never kind, she loved me without limits. She even loved my husband, J. J. Johnson who was not the right person for me. She did not judge; she did what she could and never gave a lecture. How many people can say they are that selfless?

I need to tell my older sister how much I appreciate everything she has ever done for me. She is the kind of lady with faith that models how God wants each of us to interact with people who are difficult to love. I was that person who did not love myself and there was no way I could ever love. I love Big Tae, Lil Tae, my children and family, but because of my brokenness the first sign of trouble I retreated and would not face the problems head on. Drugs, alcohol, sex and other things are what I went to, to avoid my problems. Mabel is the best. I am going to tell her right now in front of my guests.

"Mabel, can you pass the yellow gift box near you next?" I can't do it! I will tell her another time. I just want this time to be about me.

I open all the presents and envelopes and I am about to thank everyone when Tae says, "Wait, I have a present. He pulls out a long square white box and says, "This is for you." I glare at the box and the crowd says at the same time. "Open it!" The smile on my face widens as I clutch the box, opening it slowly. I see the gold charm bracelet that is very beautiful. He asks if he can put it on my lovely wrist and I move my head downward in affirmation. Everyone is watching as he gently attaches the lovely bracelet to my wrist. I thank Tae and kiss him on his jaw and he hugs me to him tightly. Tae sat close to me all night and he was he quite the gentleman.

Two months have passed and my job at the hospital as a unit secretary has been rewarding. I have been attending church and serving as a greeter twice a month. Tae comes to visit every other week. I still keep the secret about our first child from him and I need to tell him. Everything is going so well; how can or should I tell him? I don't want this wonderful time to be interrupted by telling him my oldest child is his son and that boy he never met is dead. Why should I have to disclose this small matter? I am happy and I have changed and life is good. I am going to live my life. **It's all about me!**

Mabel Johnson Pruitt
Well it is not all about you! I am Louvenia Johnson's sister Mabel Johnson Pruitt the one with the skinny legs and not so plumb rear. I will tell the real version of our home life and how, I was disliked by my family. Read the next sequel, "How can your family disown you?"

Acknowledgements

I want to thank God for selecting me, a mere human. Thank you for my parents, the late John Edward Amis and Gladys Hinton Amis and my awesome husband, Milton Louis Dickerson and our daughter Kimberly Dickerson and son Milton Amis Dickerson and my new daughter in law Rachel S. Dickerson. I also want to thank Karen Rodgers for help in editing and encouragement throughout my writing endeavor. She was patient and able to take me to a higher level on this journey called writing. I also thank Michelle Stimpson for all the marketing tips on what happens after the book is written. Last thank-you Ashley Graham and the entire staff at Lift Bridge Publishing for putting the last professional finishing touch to the book.

APPENDIX 1

The objective of the workbook is to transform individual readers through introspection and group verbal stimulation that will bring about insight to resolve internal and external problems.

Facilitator Guidelines

1. A facilitator will conduct group discussion. The facilitator should be trained in guidance/counseling or have worked in some capacity with young people. The role of the facilitator is not to teach, but to encourage group members to join the discussion, give personal views, and achieve self-awareness from the questions.
2. The facilitator must emphasize the importance of making positive statements and being sensitive to responses made by group members, as it is crucial for the overall success of the discussion.
3. The facilitator is to identify hesitant individuals and help them feel free to speak and assure them that other members of the group will be respectful and value their responses.
4. All group discussions will remain private and confidential in nature. Group members should not repeat information shared.

Group Dynamics

The completion of questions has no time limit. The facilitator will determine how much time will be needed based on the needs of participants.

Completion of all 5 Workbook questions is optional. Be flexible and complete the sessions as directed by the group's needs. The group may decide to complete less than five questions per chapter. Discussion of one chapter may take two weeks to complete or just one session. The facilitator and the group will determine the process.

Individual Instruction

The workbook contains questions that can be read and completed after completion of the corresponding book chapter. The chapter questions should be completed before meeting in a group setting. The solitary time can be completed a couple of days before the group session.

The questions asked in the discussion are to be responded to slowly, after careful consideration. Answering questions honestly will help promote individual growth through self-introspection, resulting in a journey through the maturation process. Make or purchase a notebook to journal your thoughts. You will be encouraged to write your thoughts at the conclusion of each chapter.

Chapter One: Momma's Journey to Hell and Back!

1. What happens in the closet to Louvenia? Why is it important to tell someone about the incident?

2. What does the jagged line represent that is used throughout the book?

3. Louvenia runs out of church just before giving her life to Christ. After running out of the church what did the police fail to do, consequently violating her civil rights?

4. What does the term sibling rivalry mean? Describe Mabel and Louvenia's relationship?

5. Define the term self-esteem? Describe how Louvenia struggled with the way she perceived herself. How does she feel about her teacher?

Chapter Two: Momma's Journey to Hell and Back!

1. Describe Lou's grandmother. What is your impression of her?

2. Is there a rivalry between you and one of your siblings? Do you know the root cause of the problem?

3. Think about the people in your family; is there a person who has similar character traits to Mabel's? Can you identify a friend or family member with the same mentality as the character Sammie Lee?

4. Do you have rage that escalates during certain situations? What triggers that behavior?

5. Should a person seek help for their anger problem?

Chapter Three: Momma's Journey to Hell and Back!

1. In the first two paragraphs of Chapter Three, Mabel is talking about her sister's attire. Is Mabel being helpful? Is Louvenia taking the suggestion about the dress too personally?

2. How can most of the family dislike one person in the clan? Can this kind of resentment toward a family member have a lasting effect?

3. Consider the old saying, "Absence makes the heart grow fonder." Do you think Mabel moving out of town to attend school will make the family situation better?

4. Do you think some police officers abuse their power? Share a related situation.

5. Have you ever wanted to be a part of a team or organization? What was experience like?

Chapter Four: Momma's Journey to Hell and Back!

1. What motivates you to do your best, a friend, parent or yourself?

2. Do you think Louvenia and Martavious had an instant attraction?

3. If you like a person should you show your interest, or should you play it cool for a while?

4. Have you ever daydreamed about a person you were interested in and wanted to get to know better?

5. Are you a spiritual person? Explain.

Chapter Five: Momma's Journey to Hell and Back!

1. Have you had a recent experience where you achieved or accomplished something of which you are especially proud? Briefly share the accomplishment.

2. Do you have a friend or a significant person in your life that has helped you becomes a more positive individual?

3. Have you tried studying in the library to complete assignments? Is it a beneficial place for you to study?

4. Can you ignore a person who is talking about you in a one-on-one situation or in a crowd?

5. Do you think incarcerated individuals are safe in our prison system?

Chapter Six: Momma's Journey to Hell and Back!

1. Was Mabel being thoughtful when she saved a plate of food for her sister?

2. Do you think Louvenia should try harder to be nice to her sister? Should Mabel complain or keep silent, when she makes an attempt?

3. Do you have someone in your family who abuses alcohol or drugs?

4. Are you often embarrassed by the way the abuser behaves?

5. How do you react when a family member who is under the influence verbally abuses you?

Chapter Seven: Momma's Journey to Hell and Back!

1. Should a minister or a pastor drink wine, alcohol or consume any other mind-altering substance?

2. Was the grandfather's behavior appropriate or inappropriate?

3. When you are uncomfortable with a person's un wanted touch, what should you do?

4. The "V" sign grandmother used with her fingers pointing at her husband, what was she doing when making this gesture?

5. What do you conclude was the cause of the grandfather's death? Use your detective skills. Was the grandfather a good person?

Chapter Eight: Momma's Journey to Hell and Back!

1. Have you ever felt like you were bringing shame to your family's name?

2. Have you ever been in a fight where you were double-teamed?

3. What do you think happened to make the kicking stop during the prison altercation?

4. Is gang fighting ever appropriate? Have you ever witnessed this kind of violence?

5. What should an innocent bystander do in this type of situation?

Chapter Nine: Momma's Journey to Hell and Back!

1. What emotion was Louvenia feeling when she had second thoughts about meeting Tae's family?

2. What do you do when you can't drop off to sleep?

3. Do you think pulling out a chair and standing for a lady is old school behavior? Role-play this practice.

4. Have you ever been uncomfortable in a Sunday school class, feeling inadequate because of your lack of Bible knowledge?

5. What was your impression of what Tae's father the preacher said to Louvenia?

Chapter Ten: Momma's Journey to Hell and Back!

1. Can you reflect on some behavior you have displayed that's unspeakable? Close your eyes and ask God for forgiveness.

2. In the novel Momma Said, "Hit 'Em Back!" how has Louvenia changed from that time when she visited her son in jail and talked about how he was raised to the point where she herself is a prisoner?

3. Granny Mo gives Lou some good advice about asking God to forgive her. Can you summarize what she said?

4. Why do you think Granny Mo shared her story with Lou, a story that she never shared with anyone else?

5. Do you have some images in your mind you can't seem to erase? How can you remove them?

Chapter Eleven: Momma's Journey to Hell and Back!

1. Why do you think it was hard for Louvenia to continue the good girl role?

2. What do you think about waiting until marriage to be intimate?

3. Do you know people who do not work, but always have a scheme to obtain money in an illegal way?

4. Spiking another person's drink without their permission, is it ethical?

5. Lou had a plan to seduce Tae; did she take advantage of him? What kind of emotion did the two of them display after the encounter?

Chapter Twelve: Momma's Journey to Hell and Back!

1. What kind of actions did Louvenia take right before taking the pregnancy test?

2. Do you think Louvenia was right to keep the pregnancy from Tae?

3. Do you think Tae would have changed his plans for college if he knew Lou was caring for his child?

4. Does a child have the right to know his or her father?

5. Who in a family does secrets harm fathers, children, or mothers?

Chapter Thirteen: Momma's Journey to Hell and Back!

1. Mabel wants to finish the last two months of her senior year with a friend's family, instead of changing schools. Is this a good idea?

2. Lou's mother was not a good role model. What happens to some children of this kind of parent?

3. Drinking and drugging has destroyed many families. Why do you think people can't seem to stop?

4. Eviction happens when rent is not paid to a landlord. Do you think it is right for your personal items to be thrown on the curb?

5. Lou was doing well, what happened to cause her to return back to her old life?

Chapter Fourteen: Momma's Journey to Hell and Back!

1. Louvenia was in need of medical help. Should she have let a promise she made to herself keep her from calling her family?

2. Louvenia is not use to considering other people's feelings; she usually did not care. Is this a dilemma for you?

3. If you were Mabel, based on the way her sister treated her over the years, would you help her?

4. Do you think Mabel should have remained silent when Louvenia ask how can you love a person so unlovable? What do you think she should have said to her sister?

5. Some hospitals have rumors that if you are admitted you never leave alive. Have you heard this about certain hospitals?

Chapter Fifteen: Momma's Journey to Hell and Back!

1. How did the grandmother detect that Louvenia was pregnant? Tae's father was in the clinic; do you think he suspects Louvenia is pregnant?

2. Louvenia is just told she is pregnant. Did the medical personnel disrespect her?

3. Are you surprised that Louvenia was stealing supplies in the doctor's office?

4. Louvenia's mother is in front of the store begging? How do you think she and her grandmother feel about the panhandling?

5. Louvenia watched her mother at the store. Is she destined to be just like her?

Chapter Sixteen: Momma's Journey to Hell and Back!

1. Was Louvenia showing signs of regret for the way she treated her son all his life?

2. Forgiveness can be an unbearable burden. Is there a person you can't forgive?

3. Can a person be saved outside of the church walls?

4. Can you love a person so much that when they leave through death or separation, do you think it will be difficult to love again?

5. Would you give a kidney to someone if you were known to be a match?

Chapter Seventeen: Momma's Journey to Hell and Back!

1. Should a mother ever keep a child's father's identity a secret?

2. How did Louvenia and Jack Johnson's life spiral out of control?

3. Do you believe men can't control their sexual urges?

4. Have you vowed to stop doing something that is not beneficial to your health or life?

5. Why do you think Louvenia was in disbelief about her brother?

Chapter Eighteen: Momma's Journey to Hell and Back!

1. Louvenia experienced memory loss; can you tell of an experience when someone you know has forgotten important details in their life?

2. What is the definition of dementia?

3. Do you think the medical personnel should have given Louvenia the mirror?

4. How do you think you would feel if you could not remember details about yourself?

5. Do you think praying before and after a family crisis helps?

Chapter Nineteen: Momma's Journey to Hell and Back!

1. Louvenia was depressed when she experienced memory impairment. What are the signs of depression?

2. Can a person expect to be released every time justice is not adequately served?

3. Do you believe Louvenia when she testified and said she was a changed person?

4. Are you supposed to forget about a person's past who has been released from prison?

5. Should the family as a unit all go to church and pray together?

Chapter Twenty: Momma's Journey to Hell and Back!

1. Do you agree when you are happy it is very easy to change your life?

2. When was the last time a group of people celebrated with you?

3. Do you like surprises?

4. Do you think Louvenia was happy to see Martavious?

5. Should Louvenia tell Martavious about their first child? Do you think Louvenia has really changed?

Cynthia Amis Dickerson is the author of Momma Said, "Hit 'Em Back!" her first published novel. Momma's Journey to Hell and Back! is the sequel to the first book. Cynthia is married to her husband Milton Dickerson and they reside in Memphis, Tennessee. Mrs. Dickerson is a healed breast cancer survivor of three years. God is an awesome God! She has a children's book soon to be released spring of 2016 called, Baby's First Book.